BALFOUR M2.

MGS

D1578223

The Silver Brumby
Silver Brumby's Daughter

ELYNE MITCHELL

Kingfisher Feather

ILLUSTRATED BY GRACE HUXTABLE

HUTCHINSON OF LONDON

HUTCHINSON & CO. (*Publishers*) LTD

178–202 Great Portland Street, London, W.1

London Melbourne Sydney
Auckland Bombay Toronto
Johannesburg New York

First published 1962

*This book has been set in Bembo type face. It has
been printed in Great Britain by The Anchor Press,
Ltd., in Tiptree, Essex, on Smooth Wove paper.*

For

HARRY, HONOR

and

JOHN

Contents

1 : Where the two streams meet

THERE WAS NOTHING definitely strange about the morning. It was not hot enough to make a dancing, shimmering mirage. It *was* New Year's Day, but it was just a lovely summer's morning. There was nothing unusual, no heat haze, no cloud vapour out of which a spirit or a memory could arise.

Joanna Dane and her eleven-year-old twin son and daughter, David and Sally, were riding over the paddocks of their homestead, Tiarri. 'Tiarri' means 'wind' in aborigine dialect, and the house was set out on the end of a ridge above the river bends and caught any wind that blew. They had been looking at the mares and foals; now they were getting close to the river and riding in the deep cool shade of some redgum trees. The bullocks that were camped in the shade were too lazy to move, though they watched with half-suspicious eyes.

'We'll ride to the bridge to see if a fire has been left burning by the campers,' Joanna said. 'There *is* a fire somewhere. I can smell it.'

Sally sniffed the air, turning her face to the eucalypt trees above. Her nose quivered and her forehead puckered. It was not a smell—it was just something she noticed, something different she could sense about the calm, warm day. . . .

'Come on, let's canter to the willows,' she said, shortening her reins and pressing her right leg against her pony's side. She was not running away from anything . . . she just wanted to move.

They pulled up where the willows lined the river bank—the fair-haired twins on their galloways, and their mother, also blonde with hair almost touching her shoulders—and they looked down into the deep, slow-flowing curve of the stream. Away up the river and high on a hill was the Tiarri homestead.

David looked towards the house once, thinking how he had lain in bed that morning and watched the pale blue Alps against the dawn sky; watched a flight of white cockatoos exploding, shining in a bar of sunlight, and he had felt certain that this new year must hold some great excitement for Sally and himself. Then he turned back to the slow-moving stream. This was a favourite swimming place. Across the river was a little sandy island, and, just above, was the junction of two rivers, where the Indi and the Swampy Plains became the Murray.

Joanna, the mother, was being lulled almost to sleep by the murmur of the river. This sound of the river and the sight of the water gliding by was part of her life, for she belonged to the Murray and to Tiarri as much as her husband, Alex Dane, who was also her cousin. They had lived all their lives here.

She found she was observing herself as well as her children, as though she stood apart. She noticed their blond colouring and their likeness to herself as though she was looking at it for the first time. And she too felt that everything was strange but she did not know why.

David, too, watched the flow of the water, and was beginning to feel giddy as it went by. The insistent call of an unseen rufous whistler blended with the stream's whisper. A pair of dollar birds flew up into the dome of the sky, calling their rough call and then rolling down to earth. Everything was as he had known it for years, but there was still the creeping feeling of something being different.

They rode on to the road, and came to the bridge and a stone fireplace. A fire was still smouldering. This was where the smell of burning had come from. There was no one about.

'Hitch up the horses and we'll find a tin or a billy and put that out,' Joanna Dane said. 'The country's too dry to leave a fire burning.'

They dismounted and tied their horses to the old post-and-rail fence, and scrambled through above the netting.

There were a couple of discarded tins near the fireplace.

'These'll be useful this time,' Joanna said, 'but I loathe untidy campers.' She picked up one tin and David had found a billy lying on its side in the grass. They went to the water's edge and bent down to fill them. Sally peered under the bridge at the joining of the two rivers.

Then it happened.

There was a thud, thud of a horse's hooves on the decking of the bridge, and the rumble of wheels!

Coming along the road they saw a sulky—a light two-wheeled vehicle. It was such an unusual, forgotten thing that they all three walked to the side of the bridge to see who was in it.

Sitting rather slouched on the sulky's ragged seat, and swaying with the motion, was an old lubra, an aborigine woman, in a vivid tartan skirt and a green blouse. There had been no aborigines in the Upper Murray for many, many years.

Suddenly the old woman saw the family standing there and pulled her horse up out of its jogtrot. She came on slowly, her eyes fixed on the twins. She stopped beside them, and her face creased into smiles.

'From the Dream Time,' she muttered, pointing to both Sally and David, who could not quite make out what she had said.

Joanna heard and knew that the Dream Time was, for the aborigines, a paradise of both past and future, and the home of the great spirits. She was worried that the twins might be frightened, but they were standing enchanted, smiling at the old woman.

A memory of stories of the aborigines thinking very blond white men were great spirits went quickly through Joanna's mind, but she was completely unprepared for what came next.

'Where have you come from and where are you going?' asked Sally.

The question seemed to give the old aborigine the gift of tongues.

'I am the last,' she said, 'and for many nights I have seen the white spirits. I have seen them in front of the charging red bull, chasing the mad bullock, in the path of the striking snake, on the bolting horses, by the light of the Brolga Moon when danger lies in the shadows and joy in the light, and in the great roaring waters of the flood. I have seen them in all my nights and in many places, even where the snows lie in winter, but I have never seen them at the Dragon-fly Cave.' Her voice dropped to a whisper. 'Understanding lies in the mountains, and, if you have the courage, it is in the treasures of the snow. I am the last and I have never seen you at the Dragon-fly Cave.'

The twins were puzzled. Their mother felt a queer fluttering of fear.

As though impelled to do so, David offered the old lubra a drink from the billy, holding it up to her as if it were some precious, magic liquid.

Joanna waited till she had drunk and then spoke
quickly before the old lubra could start again.

'Where are you travelling to?' she asked, but either
it was the wrong question or the water made only more
strange words spring to the lubra's tongue.

'Even spirits grow stronger if they pass through
dangers,' she said.

A little eddy of wind blew the smouldering fire, and
the smell rose around them. Joanna emptied her tin,
the water hissing on the half-burnt sticks and ashes.

'Quench the fire. Quench the fire,' the old lubra
muttered. 'The feather of the blue bird, dropped as it
flies, is the spirit's feather. I am the last, but I may yet
see you again.' Then for the first time she looked fully
at Joanna, and the likeness between Joanna and her
children must have amazed her because her eyes, under
their beetling brows, grew wide and startled.

'Swift as the wind,' she said. 'The spirits of the
Dream Time. I have seen one like you, one that went
before you, moons and moons and moons ago.'

'Where do you come from? Who are you?' Joanna
asked, almost sharply because she was filled with uneasiness, but it seemed that the gift of tongues had left
the old woman, for she said:

'Me the last of the Jillamatongs. Me bin Tumba-
rumba.' With a shake of the reins she started the horse
moving again. There was the scrunch of wheels on the
gravelled road and, surprisingly quickly, the ancient
sulky was spinning away from them bearing the shape-
less figure in the bright tartan skirt towards the Gap
and the blue sky.

'Well!' said Joanna, but she stopped speaking and waited to hear what the children had to say.

'Who was she?'

'Who could she be?'

Joanna could see that it had not yet crossed their minds that the old lubra had meant that it was they who were spirits from the Dream Time, but Sally was beginning to get puzzled.

'Mummy, *who* could she have been? She was like Dolly's and Jessie's stories of Black Mag, even to the tartan skirt. But Black Mag died years ago.'

'What did she mean?' David asked slowly. 'She seemed to think she knew who we were.'

'I don't know who she is,' Joanna answered. 'In all my lifetime there've been no aborigines here.' She knew that Sally was becoming uneasy as she thought over all the weird words the old woman had said.

They looked up the road towards the sulky that was quickly getting smaller and smaller.

'We must get on to our horses and go home, it's getting near lunch-time,' Joanna said, moving towards the fence.

David swung himself into the saddle and looked up once more.

'She's gone!' he said sharply. 'I can't see the sulky anywhere on the road.' And though they watched up and down the road, up and down, it never appeared out of the trees, as they expected it would, and they did not see it again.

2 : River glory

JOANNA AND ALEX DANE never told the twins
that, shortly after their meeting with the old aborigine,
Alex had taken the car and gone to see if he could find
her and the sulky anywhere on the road. But he never
found her.

That afternoon they went for a picnic with their
near neighbours, the Adamses. David and Sally talked
about the old woman all the way to Waterfall Farm,
right at the end of the road up the Swampy Plains
River. But just as they drove through the gate of the
farm David said:

'Don't let's say too much about her to Rickie. I don't think he'd believe it was true.' David looked rather worried. Although he did not say so, Rickie, one of the Adams boys who was near him in age, had seemed to find him rather a fool lately. The two boys had been friends, but Rickie's manner had changed since he had gone to school. 'Could we keep fairly quiet about what she said?' he added.

Joanna nodded. 'No harm done in finding out if they've seen an old lubra, though,' she said. For a while they all fell silent, wondering.

The Danes arrived before the Adamses. They stepped out of the car into the brittle, dried grass, picked up the bathing bags, and turned down the steep, bush-covered river bank.

'What a lovely smell there always is here,' said Sally, as a wave of blended, sun-hot eucalypt and prosanthera rose to meet them—the wonderful hot smell of the summer bush.

For a while the old aborigine was forgotten as they saw the green-swirling water, the white sand, the bleached piles of driftwood, the enormous, lichen-covered rocks.

'Come on, Sal,' said David, flying down the steep dusty track, his sandals slipping on the gumnuts. Then he dashed through the light and shade of the tea tree at the bottom, to a little sandy cove.

Sally joined him where he stood digging his toes into the wet sand at the water's edge, and they gazed upstream below the high suspension bridge. Suddenly it was impossible to look at it any longer without

B

wanting to leap in. They went in among the rocks, stripped off their clothes, and pulled on their bathing-suits, then dived from a rock into the translucent river.

The twins felt the sharp coldness of the water completely enfolding them. They saw, like a strange world distorted by the water, the rocks on the bottom far below them. Then they swam to the surface, gasped for breath, and saw, in the distance, the rocky outline of a ridge of Mount Townsend against the sky. By now the water did not seem so cold and they started to swim upstream.

They swam a rhythmic, swift crawl, like arrows speeding up the river. They passed a little cove, where their father and mother were standing, and began to feel the force of the current against them.

'You'll need to hug the side to get up against that current,' Joanna called. 'Come in here and wait for us, we're coming.'

The twins allowed themselves to drift into the bay and lay there roasting in the sun while their parents changed. A little copper-coloured lizard crept along a piece of driftwood, watching them beadily. Almost quicker than one could see, it caught a fly and then vanished back into the bush.

'Come on! Race you all!' Joanna called, and the four raced to the water and plunged in.

'Keep close to the rocks and follow your mother. She knows the way upstream like a salmon,' Alex Dane shouted.

As they swam under the swing-bridge the river became narrower and swifter with steep, vertical rocks on one side, and great, flat slabs of rock on the other. The main current was in the centre.

Following their mother, the twins swam close to the rock cliffs, and each time they turned their heads for a breath they saw into little dark caves where you could imagine crayfish creeping in and out—where the snow waters of the floods would roar in the spring.

David looked into the last cave, but he didn't turn his head back to breathe out again because he saw something that gave him a shock. He saw the distorted image of a face in the water of the cave. Quickly he realized it was a reflection, and looked up at the high rocks above. Standing by a ribbon gum that grew out of the cliff, and looking down at him, was the old aborigine woman. For a moment their eyes met, then she seemed to fade away.

By this time David was left far behind and, bewildered though he was, he hurried to join the others. They had reached a point where the river was split by a big triangular rock, and the two arms of current boiled together just below it. His mother, father and Sally were standing on a rock beside the stream. Above the great rock in the middle the stream was narrow, swift and deep.

David hurried to join them, but said nothing about the old woman because his mother was standing on a shelf of rock, ready to spring across the current.

'Look carefully,' she said, tossing the wet hair out of her eyes. 'This swift current is not coming straight down on to you, but across, to meet the other arm of the stream. Above where they meet, and below the rock, there is a backwater: once you get into it, it almost sucks you upstream to the rock.'

Sally whistled.

'We'll have to swim terribly hard across that strip of current to get into the backwater!'

'That's it,' her father said. 'And, if you don't make it, go downstream on to the opposite side and get out on the low rocks.'

'Wait till I wave you on before you come,' Joanna said. She pushed off from the ledge as hard as she could, into the rushing stream, head tucked into the water, legs scissoring, arms pulling. Then she was through. She swam easily up to the rock, gripped it and stood on the slippery, submerged boulders.

'Come on,' she called, and one after another Sally, David and their father sprang into the current and swam furiously across till they reached the calmer water and the big rock.

They sat on the rock, and David was just going to say something about the old aborigine appearing and vanishing like a fading film in the bright day, when he saw his mother's face suddenly change. She sat upright and looked towards the cliffs above. He turned his head in the same direction as hers and saw the lubra's figure again. This time she had one arm raised, pointing to the mountains. As he looked, she began to fade away.

'Mummy!' he said sharply. 'I'm sure she means that we must find something or learn something in the mountains.'

'Who?' said Sally and their father.

'The same aborigine woman. She appeared for a moment on the rock cliff,' said Joanna slowly.

'Where?' asked Sally.

'I saw her before,' said David. 'That's why I was late up the river. I saw her reflection in the water as I passed the last cave, then I looked up and saw her.'

'There's the Adamses' car coming,' Alex Dane said. They could all hear it, but not one of them moved.

Then, further down, they saw Mrs. Adams walking out along the swing-bridge, and heard her calling to them. Just then each one of the Danes saw the old lubra again, further down the cliffs. She flung out her arm, urgently pointing towards the mountains, then suddenly she vanished.

'Why are you all looking as if you'd seen a ghost?' Jane Adams called. 'Come on down. Happy New Year to you!'

'Happy New Year,' they called, and dived off the rock, swimming down the cold, green stream. The twins could hardly look forward any longer to a rough-and-tumble afternoon. Their heads were empty of everything except the vision of the old aborigine on the cliff.

'Perhaps no one sees the aborigine except us,' Joanna thought as she went fast through the current.

Down on the beach, the Adams family had sorted out bathing-suits and children. Rickie and Margaret, the two who were closest to the twins in age, were changing in the rocks when the Danes swam into the cove.

David suddenly found he had ceased to worry

about Rickie's superiority. The river flowed beside him,
there were the sun-baked rocks, the smell of the bush:
and he felt his own strength—felt his strength as one with
the river, the sun and the bush. There was nothing to
worry about. And ahead, mysteriously, there must be
adventure. What else could the old woman mean?

'Let's go!' he said, and turning to Sally, he added:
'Up the river, then over to the rocks we've just come
from.' Then, as they ran into the water, he whispered
to her: 'Queer how more ghostly and fading she was
than this morning.'

'Yes,' Sally whispered back, and they both dived in.

Rickie and Margaret, brown-haired and rather
more solid than the tall, thin twins, followed them.

David led the way, hugging close to the cliffs and
going as high up the stream as he could because he
wanted to look into that cave again. But when he got
there he saw no water-rippled reflection of a face.

When he stopped and felt with his feet for the
ledge Sally was close beside him, Rickie a few lengths
back and Margaret struggling along behind.

'Wait for Margaret,' said Sally. She really liked the
Adamses. Rickie had not been very nice to David
lately, but surely here he would be nicer. He could not
try to organize them all to play cricket in this place,
where the river sang its continual invitation.

'We'll give you a chance to get your breath, Margie,
before we set off again. Anyway, the next lap is downstream to those rocks.'

'I'm all right now,' said Margaret.

'Well, away, away!' cried David, hurling himself

into the current, hurtling down the stream, feeling somehow that he must swim his best in case the old aborigine woman was watching.

Sally was barely a second behind, then Rickie and Margaret, easily water-borne, yet lacking in some essential drive that was possessed by Sally and David. They all pulled themselves out on to the rocks and went back over the hot, white sand, jumping from one patch of shade to another, to look at the heaps of grey drift-wood, whittled and water-worn into strange shapes.

'I wonder where each piece has come from?' David said.

'Here's one shaped like a boomerang and almost polished.' Rickie stooped and picked it up off the heap.

David held out his hand for the piece of wood.

'May I see it for a moment?' He took it, standing poised as though to throw. 'I've often wanted a real boomerang,' he said.

Rickie scowled.

'You'd never be able to throw it if you had. You can't even throw a ball.' This statement was only too true.

'Oh, Rickie!' said Margaret.

'Listen, Rickie,' Sally said. 'The aborigines couldn't throw a ball either, and what does being able to throw, and catch, or kick a ball, matter here?'

'You're just a silly girl,' said Rickie. 'It matters an awful lot.'

'What good is a ball to you in the river, in the snow, or on a horse, or alone in the bush?' Sally asked firmly.

'You talk nonsense,' Rickie's voice was contemptuous. 'You just don't know what it's like to play in a team.'

'No,' David still stood ready to throw, 'but——'

'Oh, stow it!' said Sally. 'It's New Year's Day, and too nice to argue.' She thought that perhaps Rickie, even if he was good at games, was jealous of David, but she could feel her twin's confidence seeping away.

'I bet you'd never have the guts, if anyone challenged you to do something really dangerous, to set to and do it,' Rickie said.

David suddenly wondered how good he would be at taking up a challenge, and he threw the driftwood in a high curve through the air.

Joanna, down in the cove near the beach, holding Elizabeth—the youngest Adams daughter—by the ribs as she tried to dog-paddle, looked up and saw the tense group of children. She saw David fling the boomerang, and realized that they were about to quarrel.

'Time for you to sun-bathe,' she told Elizabeth, and said to Jane Adams: 'I'm going to take the children up to the rapids.' Then she swam straight up the river, pulling herself out on to the rocks in the lovely hot beat of the sun.

'Come on up the rock slabs,' she called, 'and let ourselves into the swift water below the rapids,' and she led them off, leaping from one hot slab to another, balancing on small ribs of rock over little sandy rifts, scrambling up to the largest rock above the rapids. She stood looking into the boiling, foaming stream down which she had often swum, as though she was looking into her memories of the mountains up above, of streams and waterfalls, of the Blue Lake, of Lake Albina. The children stood beside her and she wondered if some day they would possess memories like these. At least now she would give them the memory of hurtling down in the swift water, of hard swimming which would need a strength and skill that they would not have possessed last year.

'How beautiful the deep green curve of it is, the bubble and the foam,' she said, and climbed down into shallow, calm water at the foot of the rock, followed by the children.

Round she edged, just keeping out of the rushing stream that would tear them from footholds or hand-holds, up on to a great water-hollowed granite shelf, smooth, polished like marble and, where it was below the surface of the water, extremely slippery. From here it should not be beyond the skill of the children to let themselves slide in and be hurtled down the current, though it was further up the stream than they had ever been before, and the water seemed unusually high and swift.

Joanna stood on the edge, one foot rubbing over a smoothed hollow where perhaps the granite must have been softer and, over many years, worn out by the water, then she looked thoughtfully at the children. Her own two were quite capable of sliding safely into the current. She walked down the marble shelf to its lower end.

'Come here, Margie,' she said. 'When I whizz past,

you go in from here. I'll start from the top and the others can follow me.'

David and Sally both thought together—as they often did—that this, in its way, was a small challenge, to swim strongly so that the current could not sweep them on to the rocks, and perhaps to swim better than the more robust Rickie and Margaret. Then they were in the whirling, swirling water, arms and legs made almost powerless by its force—almost powerless but not quite, because they found they could still swim and go in the direction in which they intended.

The twins reached the calm water before the Adamses, then all four flung themselves on the hot sand, laughing, talking, so pleased with themselves that any trouble was forgotten.

Brian Adams and Alex Dane were under a tea tree talking about cattle and the Snowy Mountain Scheme which was changing the whole of the Australian Alps where once both families used to run cattle in the snow-leases. The others joined them and lay on the hot sand. Suddenly in a lull in the talk and laughter there was a raucous chattering sound from a nearby ribbon gum.

Sally raised her head from her folded arms.

'There's a kingfisher somewhere,' she said, and she and David both sat up, looking all around them.

Then it flashed out, flying across the river, bright lacquered blue wings and back, shining white collar, shining white breast. It dipped once towards the river— the white almost touching the luminous water—and then went on, to vanish in the tea tree on the far side.

'A kingfisher for the New Year,' said Joanna.

'What was it you read to us, Mummy, about a kingfisher?' Sally asked.

' "When the kingfisher's wing answers light to light and is silent," ' her mother answered. 'You know, it is strange that we've never seen a kingfisher's feather on the ground.'

David sat up suddenly again.

'A kingfisher's feather! That must be the feather of the blue bird that she mentioned.' His eyes were wide open and he had forgotten that he had not meant to say anything about the aborigine woman.

Joanna spoke quietly:

'Haven't seen an old lubra dressed in a tartan skirt, driving a sulky, have you, Jane?'

'No,' Jane Adams answered. 'I haven't seen an aborigine for years, and that one sounds like Black Mag. She must have been dead for fifty years or more. She was supposed to be the last of the Jillamatongs.'

'My father had a story,' said Brian Adams to Joanna, 'that Black Mag told him, when he was a small boy, that your grandfather had come back from the Alcheringa, the Dream Time. Of course your grandfather was an exceptional man for his time, respecting and understanding the aborigines as he did. And he learnt about the bush from them as though he were a native of the land, not just first generation born here.'

'Did he really know the bush as they did?' David asked.

'He couldn't really have known it as well, but he was believed to have done by everyone who lived around.'

3 : Call to adventure

BELOW TIARRI'S HILL the paddocks lay bleached in that colourless light before the night, bleached to an off-white, drawn over by the brown lines of fences, the darker crescents of lagoons and the dense forms of red-gums. The land was stripped of the day and the day's activities—stripped down to its own essential self.

Darkness would come soon. Soon there would be the last sleepy warble of the magpies, a final burst of kookaburra laughter. The possums and the mopokes would take over, but now, against the dying light in the sky, Sally turned catherine-wheels on the lawn.

David lay on the grass and, further along, Joanna and Alex sat watching Sally, talking, half dreaming. They had enjoyed the picnic, and were pleasantly sleepy. Joanna kept thinking of the morning's strange meeting, turning it all over in her mind.

'We *must* have seen her,' she said, half aloud. 'We couldn't all have imagined her.'

'Yes, we certainly saw her,' Alex said, 'but I'd love to know where she got to and who she is. I wouldn't worry, though, about what she said.'

'Queer the change of language—the good Queen's English and then the drop into pidgin.'

'It's true, what Brian said about our grandfather,' Alex went on. 'I don't mean that he came back from the Dream Time, the Alcheringa, but about his sympathy with the aborigines, the understanding of the bush.'

'She must have meant him when she said "one that went before you".' Joanna moved restlessly. It was as though something important had entered into their lives that morning—and yet perhaps it was rather ridiculous to believe that it had happened. *They* had seen her again this afternoon, but Jane Adams had not. Joanna felt her skin creeping slightly, but whatever it all meant, and if it was indeed a mystery, it was a mystery that had grown out of the land, the water, the very air which surrounded them. And, if she doubted her eyes and ears, the twins believed implicitly that the old woman existed.

Sally went on turning, whirling, performing a dance to the departing light. At last, exhausted, she flung herself down by her twin, and it seemed that the day had suddenly gone, and the last bird winged across the sky.

They all became aware that the Southern Cross was twinkling above the mountains, and with the darkness came the whispering south wind bearing the thrilling scent of the mountain eucalypts.

Joanna threw her head back and drew in a deep breath.

'Inhaling the mountains in one gulp?' Alex laughed at her.

David sat up and asked:

'When can we go to "the tops", Mummy?'

'Soon,' she replied. 'As soon as we are sure that the snowgums are flowering.'

'And that,' said his father, 'might be now, though I can't smell them yet, so we'll go any day. This year there should be a wonderful flowering.'

'Perhaps we'll go in three or four days' time,' Joanna said, 'and it's bedtime now.'

'Tomorrow,' Alex's voice sounded remote and sleepy, 'we must get four truck-loads of bullocks ready for market.'

'Oh, good!'

'Where from?' The twins' voices were eager.

'Take the best from the Loop Paddock.'

'Should be a lovely day.' Joanna put an arm across the shoulders of each twin and took them with her towards the door. 'It really is bedtime,' she said.

The twins went to their beds by those windows which hung over space, and through which the bright stars of the Southern Cross pointed the way to the land of the brumbies, to Dead Horse Gap, to Groggin, to the Cascades, to Quambat Flat and the Pilot.

As they were sinking to sleep, Buckwong, David's pony, neighed, down in the horse paddock. David heard the well-known sound from where he was already, in that queer, moving, shadowy borderland between sleeping and waking, and he thought the horse was calling him, eagerly saying: 'Come on! Come on!' and he smiled.

Joanna, hearing, thought how the neigh of a horse in the night sounded like a call to adventure ringing out through the dark.

4 : Red bull with the wicked eye

WHIS—s—s! A wood duck, whirring, whistling, flew out from under the rough wooden bridge that crossed a runner, a deep waterway that filled from the river. Buckwong's hooves clattered and slid as he shied nearly over the side of the bridge. David felt his stomach and thigh muscles tighten, knew that the leaves of a willow had touched his shoulder and cheek, heard his own breath come out in a whistle as the pony only just held his feet.

With a rattle like thunder on the wood, Buckwong bounded off the bridge, and the sweat which had broken on David's face and neck went cold.

'Close go!' said Sally. 'Gosh, you'd have made a splash! Mummy may be right when she says she hates riding over this bridge.'

Buckwong was shaking.

'Now he'll be ready to shy at everything,' said David, and a minute later the black pony gave a wild leap to one side, away from a stick that moved under his feet. He landed with his four feet widely spread, and snorted with fear.

Sally saw the fiery red of the inside of Buckwong's nostrils, noticed the white of his eye showing, his black coat shining with sweat. She could feel her own pony, The Banjo, being infected with his nervousness.

David grinned. The day might provide more fun than they had bargained for. He, too, would be tense now, probably for the rest of the morning, and both he and Sally knew it.

'I'll be almost as ready to shy as Buckwong,' he chuckled.

The musterers were meeting at the furthest river point and then spreading out each way along the river from there. The twins were alone at this moment only because they had wanted to follow a big runner along to the bridge, hoping to see an azure kingfisher that was sometimes there. They had seen no kingfishers, and David had nearly sailed off the bridge. Now they cantered across the paddock, out in the bright sun.

There were gutters to cross that were filled with high tussocks over which the ponies stumbled. Behind some reeds a heap of white ibis feathers lay where a

C

fox had had a meal. Buckwong shied wildly again and
The Banjo shied in sympathy. Sally began to laugh.
She felt her pony trembling between her knees, and
she was shaking too. Suddenly under their hooves, with
a whirr-r-r, five quail shot up. Both ponies propped
instantly, their legs going in every direction. David
just managed to pull himself back into the saddle.

'It only wants a darn' snake to sit up and hiss at us
and we'll jump out of our skins,' Sally laughed.

No snake even let itself be seen in the tussocks and
no more birds flew up. There were only shadows to
shy at and ibis to watch, writing a pattern in the sky,
but the ponies remained tensely on their toes, even when
they had joined the other musterers down near the big
point.

Their mother and father were there already. Joanna
looked at the twins and frowned. Their help was needed
because this was a big paddock to muster. There were
several tussocky, scrubby river points, also thick, overhanging willows all along the river banks, hollows and
bogs, and deep, dry lagoon beds where the sleepy fat
bullocks could hide. The twins and their ponies were
obviously on edge. Joanna opened her mouth to ask
them what was the matter, but Alex was already
sending them off, up the river, round all the points and
bends, to work the cattle in towards the centre of the
paddock, and then up the paddock in the direction of
the gate. Joanna and their stockman, old Jackie, were
to go down the river.

'Twins seem a little edgy,' she said to Alex.

Alex had been thinking too much of the cattle to

notice. He looked at them now, as they rode away in their old straw hats, their whips coiled in their right hands.

'I'll be quite close, and I'll watch them,' he said. 'Ponies seem rather on their toes.'

Joanna, telling herself not to be silly, went off with old Jackie, down the long point. Alex followed the twins.

The twins rode on in the hot sunshine, the exciting muster ahead, and the feeling that there was something more than that waiting for them and for their ponies. Something waited for them here by the river, where the white ibis roosted, where they rarely rode without seeing a long, sinuous tiger-snake glide among the reeds, where in winter a fox might run through the frosted tussocks.

The tussocks were swishing against their legs now, as they went down the narrow point. Beside them there was a lagoon where once, not long ago, the river had run. Four black swans were floating on the water. They turned their long necks and watched the children for a few moments before suddenly starting to run along the surface, their wings, surprisingly white, flailing the water as they ran, bright spray flashing, till they took off and flew. The ponies watched, trembling. They had seen this sight often, but they trembled now because every movement around them seemed to foretell danger.

David saw what looked like a heavy patch of shade below the willows resolve itself into red hides, horns, swishing tails.

'Some beasts right down on the river, there,' he said.

Sally pushed her straw hat back from her hot forehead and slouched a little in the saddle while they gently drove the seven beasts along the point.

'Going to be hot before we're finished.'

David steadied Buckwong as he stumbled over an unseen log in the tussocks.

'M'm, but even the heat isn't going to quieten these ponies down, and the bullocks will be lazy.' He watched a dollar bird rolling in the dome of the sky.

There were more great red beasts lying under some willows that grew below the high river bank, and four or five more under a redgum, standing where the camp-grass was still green, flicking the flies with their red and white tails. David and Sally moved them all on, slowly and without any trouble. Their father was quite close, with a small mob of cattle. The twins drove the cattle towards him before turning back to go down the next point.

Several large redgums grew close together in this point, and scrub bushes below them. Cattle had made tunnels in the bushes, but these were prickly tracks for a horse and rider. The twins went round the outside of the thicket, saying 'Get up there!' and lightly cracking their whips. No beasts came out. They reined in and listened. Undoubtedly there were one or two bullocks moving around inside. David cracked his whip more commandingly. There came a snort from in among the scrub and great trunks of redgums, but not a bullock came. They rode round looking for the least prickly tunnel. David saw one that seemed wider and higher, and rode into it. Buckwong did not want to go in and David had managed to force him between only the first prickly branches when he saw a tremendous red head, a wicked small eye and the horns of what must be a shorthorn bull. It was coming straight towards him.

This was what Buckwong had been waiting for! Something had told him that this was to be. He swung round and away. The bull bellowed and charged out of the scrub after him.

Sally saw first David and Buckwong, then the huge red roan bull shooting past her. She dug her heels into The Banjo and went after the bull, galloping, galloping, in terror that Buckwong would put his foot in a hole and fall.

David was trying to stop Buckwong or swing him to one side, but the pony was mad with fear. Twice he stumbled and only just recovered himself. Sally could see that the bull had gained with each stumble—but *she* was gaining on the bull.

She leant forward in the saddle and urged The Banjo on over the uneven tussocky ground. The Banjo's head came level with the bull's huge quarters and Buckwong was only three lengths ahead. Then Sally herself was passing the bull's quarters, passing his shoulders. She swung up her light whip. As she galloped alongside the bull she cracked it across its eyes, swung it up again and, with all her strength, brought it down and across them once more.

The bull shook its head, went on a few strides, then stopped and bellowed, and started pawing the ground. Sally, suddenly terrified, heard her father's voice but not his words. All she could see was the menacing head, the nostrils snorting into the ground as the forefoot dug into the ground. She did not know where to go or what to do. The whole day, the whole world, was filled with the one huge, pawing, snorting, angry bull.

David succeeded in swinging Buckwong round and was galloping back towards her, but she could not see him. Her father was galloping towards her too, cracking his heavy whip as he came, but she did not see him either. Then the bull must have heard Buckwong, his first quarry, because he raised his head, bellowing defiance, and began slowly to advance to meet him, swinging his head, roaring.

David swung to one side, thinking they must try to drive the bull over the river. His whip was no heavier than Sally's, and the bull would barely feel it. He cracked it as hard as he could, hoping the noise of it might check the beast, but suddenly it was as though there was an echo of whip-cracks coming on, louder and louder. Like a whirlwind, his father arrived, cracking his heavy whip all around the bull.

The bull gathered itself together to charge the dancing bay horse. The horse stepped nimbly out of the way and down came the whip. Then Alex Dane was behind the roan, driving him, flogging him.

'We'll put him in with the mob and he'll probably go along better,' he said. 'Come on! Drive him!' He looked at the white-faced twins. The whole incident had taken little more than a minute, but it had been a bad minute. 'You did very well. Come on, we'll have to keep him going.'

David was looking at the bull.

'Daddy, where's he come from? He's not ours, and he hasn't come from over the river—he hasn't got their brand.'

'You're quite right. I don't recognize the brand or ear-mark. Anyway, we'll have to take him to the yards. Can't leave an ill-tempered chap like him loose.'

'Here comes Mummy,' said Sally.

'Now she *couldn't* have heard the whip very loudly from where she was mustering,' Alex thought, giving the bull another cut around the legs because it looked as if it might stop. Then he said aloud: 'Must keep him going. If he stops he could be very difficult,' and to himself he added: 'It's just what the old aborigine said—in front of the charging red bull . . . how very queer. She said a lot of other things too . . . a mad bullock . . . a striking snake——'

Just then the bull saw Joanna coming and, with a bellow, put his head down and galloped straight towards her.

Alex touched his bay horse with his spurs and it leapt forward. The twins both saw their mother move her whip and collect her small brown stock pony so that it was well in hand. They, too, shot forward after the bull.

David had always known that Buckwong, though perhaps not so nimble on his feet as The Banjo, was very fast. Now, to his horrified astonishment, he found he was going faster than his father, faster than the bull. It would be *he* who would have to stop the beast!

'Golly!' he muttered to himself. 'Oh, golly!'

Like Sally, he rode up on the bull's near side. Like Sally, he brought his whip lashing down across the animal's face—and made no impression. The bull was getting very close to his mother now, and she was still cantering towards it. Then Joanna cracked her whip loudly. The bull checked. Alex was suddenly there, on the bull's off side.

'Come on!' he shouted. 'We must run him into the mob while we've got him. Come on, Joanna! Come on, Sal! Get behind and drive him, and David and I will keep him going straight.'

The bull was given no chance to let up till he was almost in the mob. They let him go the last fifty yards on his own, hoping not to disturb their fat cattle too much.

The four Danes sat on their horses and watched him lumbering over the dark rye grass and into the mob.

'I'll have to keep an eye on this chap now,' said Alex to Joanna, 'and you and the twins muster the rest of this half of the paddock. Jackie will manage all right on his own.'

'I hope he will,' Joanna answered. 'Anyway, once we get this half done, we can go and help him.'

'I'll keep the mob moving up the paddock,' Alex said, 'and you can add to it as you drive the beasts away from the river.'

The twins and their mother turned towards the river again. The ponies were still touchy, shying at everything, but the rest of the muster went easily. It followed the usual pattern of summer musters—they sought out the lazy red beasts in every patch of shade and rode behind them as they moved ponderously across the paddock. They heard the muted warble of magpies when the day grew hotter, and the clear, repeated whistle of the whistling eagles as the birds floated above in the bright blue sky.

David and Sally looked with longing at the river, and their mother, knowing their thoughts, laughed and said:

'We will swim when everything is over—probably in the lagoon.'

They rode on without talking a great deal, quietly moving all the cattle in towards the mob. Finally they reached the last of the river points where floods always cast the bleached driftwood high, and where the lines of the spring's receding waters could still be seen in thick curves of sticks, and tussock grass, and leaves. Then they were back at the runner, where it came out of the river, near the bridge on which the day's excitement had started. Soon the cattle would be through the gate into the next paddock, and there they would be held in a corner, the fats cut out for market, the bull driven off to the yards. Sally and David were hot and dusty, but the heat and the tiredness seemed to blow away as the mob were counted through the gate and going up the fence to the corner. Now would come the tense excitement of riding into the mob one at a time, beside either of their parents, feeling their knees bumping against a bullock's flank or even sometimes against a wide, raking horn, then hearing their father's voice say: 'That red beast, there. Cut him out!' and looking

at the moving mob of red backs and praying for enough
sense to know which one he meant!

'Come with me, David.' That was what they had
been waiting to hear.

David rode into the mob beside his father, almost
holding his breath with excitement.

'There we are. There are two near the outside which
will do us. See, those two red ones there.'

David looked along the wing of the seething red
mob. He and Sally often laughed together at the way
their father said 'that red one', but the job was too
serious for him to laugh now. He stuck close to his
father, watching every move he made, and every move
of the bullocks. Gradually, two bullocks seemed to
move ahead of the others and a little out from the mob,
and it seemed more as if they moved by force of his
father's will than by anything he did to them.

'Now!' said Alex. 'You take the outside one.'

Even then they moved quietly. David, with his
eyes glued to his red beast, blocked it from swinging
back into the mob, and then cantered after it along the
fence. His mother moved in to cut both the bullocks
off from the mob.

Sally was near her mother, her face eager. They
went forward together to get the next beasts, riding
silently into the mob, looking at each beast from
behind. Joanna and Alex Dane knew the bullocks so
well that they had already decided on quite a number of
those they were intending to send to market.

Sally threaded her way through the mob beside her
mother. The cattle were already settling down and

not wedging together so tightly. Joanna pointed her whip at the beast Sally was to cut out, and moved on to another one herself.

Sally rode quietly alongside hers without letting The Banjo's nose get further forward than its quarters. The bullock moved and she kept up with it. It looked round at her, then swung the other way. The Banjo, on his toes, swung quietly too, so that the beast turned back again and went the way Sally was trying to drive it. She saw her mother's bullock going through the mob too, and worked hers up towards it. Soon they would be able to run them both out together.

The work went on while the morning grew hotter and hotter. At last Alex said to the twins:

'I think that's right, but go and count them.'

The twins cantered off, passing old Jackie, who laughed at them and warned them to make the count right.

'Wonder how many there should be?' David muttered.

'Anything between forty and forty-four,' Sally answered.

'Of course! Four trucks. These are pretty big bullocks.'

Then they were riding slowly along the strung-out cattle.

'Two, four, six, eight . . .'

'I get forty-three,' said David, frowning, 'but I think I may have counted one twice.'

'Seems like it. I get forty-two. Count again on the way back.'

Slowly they rode back down the line. The red and white beasts were grazing and not difficult to count.

'Forty-two it is,' said David.

'Yes, I get it again.'

They announced their count when they got back to the others.

'Forty-two should be right,' their father said. 'Now for Billy the Bull.' He was just turning to ride back into the mob when Sally's voice rang out excitedly.

'Mummy! He was the charging red bull that Black Mag, or whoever she was, mentioned. Do you think all the other things she talked about will happen to us?'

Joanna looked startled and disconcerted for a moment.

'Better find a kingfisher feather to bring you luck,' she said, and she laughed so that her words seemed like only a joke.

'What comes next?' said Sally, and no one could remember what the old woman had said next, or, if Joanna did, she did not say.

'What next? What next?' Sally chanted.

'The next real excitement is a day in the mountains when the snowgums are flowering,' said David, 'and perhaps we may find Dragon-fly Cave.'

'Perhaps we shall see brumbies!' said Sally.

5 : To the land of the brumbies

A FEW DAYS went by with nothing else to remind the Dane family of the words that were spoken where the two streams meet. Each day the weather was hot and clear, and the paddocks were getting drier. Each night a cool, drying south wind blew from the mountains down the valley to Tiarri. The rhythm of their summer life went on.

The night wind moved the curtains in the office where Joanna and Alex were working over their sheep-books. Joanna turned up her face to its cold touch and then said thoughtfully:

'We should give the twins their day in the mountains before it gets so dry that we are too worried about fires to leave the place. Don't you think it would be an idea to go tomorrow?'

Alex grunted.

'We were going to drench sheep—the two-tooths.'

'I know, but one day wouldn't make much difference.'

'I suppose not,' Alex answered and sat thinking for a moment. 'Oh yes, let's,' he said.

Both of them were thinking of that wild, lonely country through which no road passed, where they used to muster cattle in summer and ski in winter; they were thinking of snow covering everything and wind crying through the snowgums.

Then a worried look spread over Joanna's face.

'Oh, blow!' she said. 'Jane asked me most particularly if we would take Rickie and Margaret when we went. Isn't that maddening!'

'What a nuisance,' said Alex. 'Never mind, we can take ours on their own another time, when Rickie and Margie are at school.'

Joanna nodded.

'I wish there didn't seem to be a sort of tension between David and Rickie now, one always trying to prove himself better than the other.'

'M'm. Don't worry. It will soon pass. Ring up Jane, then I'll help you get everything ready. Let's leave early. By the way, I don't know why I forgot to tell you, but that bull was travelling to be sold. Came from Baxter's. He'll be sausages soon. Probably give a few people bad dreams!'

Joanna was already talking to Jane Adams on the telephone, and Alex, still thinking of the bull, heard her say: '. . . windcheaters and bathers . . .' and saw in his mind a jumble containing a red bull, the white face of his daughter, windcheaters, bathers, the river redgums of the flats and the beloved outline of the mountains.

Joanna was still speaking:

'Tell them not to expect a wonderful picnic. We've only just decided to go. . . . Alex is talking about a bull. I think we'll take sausages. . . . Oh, right, if you've really got them to spare. . . . See you at seven, then.' She rang off and turned to Alex. 'Jane's got some egg-and-bacon tarts,' she said. 'We must start getting things ready. I only hope the two boys won't be in opposition all day, and David too taken up by it to enjoy all we are going to see and do.'

'No, I'm sure they won't. Everyone will enjoy it. It will be lovely to be up on the tops again, and the immense mountains will stop the boys fighting. Anyway, I had a feeling at Waterfall Farm that David wasn't worried by Rickie.'

'I'm not at all certain. But come on, let's get things ready.'

Alex felt a lightness in his steps as he followed her to the kitchen. They would be up in the mountains— in the country which was part of themselves. The country which they felt to be their own, even if they no longer ran cattle there, even if bulldozers, great earth-movers, tractors and the scars of roads had partly destroyed the utter wildness, partly destroyed the remote and infinitely ancient quality of Australia's mysterious mountains.

He knew that Joanna felt the same, and felt the same gladness that they had known these mountains before ever the roads and dams, the pipelines and hydro-electricity stations were planned. The children would not really know what they had missed, though they might regret that their expeditions into Geehi had been made by car and not winding through the bush following a mob of cattle, waiting eagerly for the first thrilling sight of the Alps from the top of the Geehi Wall.

For Alex and Joanna could remember many camps in that secret, enclosed place which was Geehi—the Alps rising in front of them, and the Geehi Wall behind; the river rushing past the hut; no roads except the winding cattle tracks; no bridges except the swinging footbridge just below the entry of the Geehi Creek. Even their parents had not been among the first people to find Geehi. Count Strezlecki had gone that way when he climbed the mountains in 1840, over a hundred years ago. Alex, when he was small, used to dream how exciting it must have been to be the first—the first to look into that lovely hidden place below the Alps, the first to climb up the steep western face and look back into the Murray Valley.

Joanna was packing up biscuits, butter, tinned pineapple, oranges, tomatoes, cake, a billy, tea, matches.

'I'll grill the sausages while we get ready tomorrow morning,' she said, and in both their ears was the roar of the wind down the snowgum glades.

*   *   *   *   *

Sally was just waking when Joanna came in, fully dressed, in the cool dawn-time.

'What is it, Mummy?' she asked, sitting up quickly.

'We're going up the mountains. The snowgums must be flowering.'

'Oh, lovely, lovely!' Sally bounced on her bed.

David stirred and woke.

'Dead Horse Gap?' he asked, almost as his eyes opened.

Joanna smiled.

'Yes, Dead Horse Gap. Put on jodhpurs: it will be cooler up there, and anyway your legs will get too scratched in shorts, and you'll need jerseys. Hurry! Breakfast will be ready soon.' She went out and left them diving into drawers to find their clothes. Then she called back through the door: 'Desert boots. You'll be glad of their rubber soles, and don't forget your dark glasses.'

Sally jumped on to the table and did a wild dance, then flung herself into her clothes.

'A clean shirt,' she chanted, 'in honour of the mountains, and my old blue jersey.'

'Let's wear our cowboy belts.'

'Yes, let's.' Sally was skipping round the room.

Joanna, hearing them, smiled and sighed. She was glad that they were so pleased to be going, but this over-excitement was very exhausting and so there had been fewer mountain expeditions than there might have been. Rickie and Margaret would last the day far better. When it was all over they would have seen less, imagined less, felt less, but they would also be far less tired.

D

'In the end it will work out all right,' Joanna told herself hopefully, as she had done for years, from the first, when she was confronted with the twin babies who screamed and screamed after they were taken picnicking. They came rushing down now, all correct, from desert boots to jerseys.

Everything was ready—only the breakfast had to be eaten while the dawn filtered into the dining-room.

'We're taking Rickie and Margaret,' Joanna said.

'Oh, blow!' said Sally, but David sat quietly. At last he said:

'I wish Rickie was not so strong . . . or perhaps he just doesn't like me any more. He always manages to set me a test. . . .' Then he began to laugh. 'Talk of passing through dangers! Everyone is after us, from old aborigine women to our own neighbours!'

Soon they were piling into the Land Rover, out at the back by the hitching-posts where Joanna and Alex had saddled and loaded their pack-horses not so very long ago.

'You drive out and I'll drive home,' Alex said.

Joanna slid in behind the wheel, then she put the lever into first gear, and they were away. On their left was the mountain skyline to which they were going—more than a day's ride, but only a little over two hours in the Land Rover on the Snowy Mountain Authority's Alpine Way. She felt the bubbling excitement of the twins filling the car.

At the Adamses' homestead they were greeted by the barking of many dogs and the children coming through the bright early morning, the magpies carolling high in the redgums. Mrs. Adams came out with the baby on her hip.

The Dane family scrambled out of the Land Rover. Rickie and Margaret were standing looking important. Elizabeth was envious.

'We mustn't stay,' said Alex. Then they were all in the Land Rover, the others waving goodbye.

When David looked back Elizabeth was already running off towards the kennels, and he could see that her mother was calling. He bet himself that she was saying: 'Come back, don't get dirty before breakfast!'

In a few minutes they turned off the old road and headed into the bush.

This bush, almost all the way to the Geehi Wall, is quiet, nearly drab, yet for anyone who has, as Joanna and Alex Dane had, travelled its winding cattle tracks or ridden out with skis slung on their shoulders, the great, silent, white mountains the goal ahead, that bush is vested with an excitement blended of memories and anticipation.

Joanna stopped the Land Rover as the road turned on to the Wall, as the hillside of blanketwood and wattles dropped away suddenly, steeply. There in front of them were the soaring mountains, still with a little snow drifted in crevices across the blue.

The children got out to stand on the edge of the drop. David looked across the steepness to the high, rugged mountains from which they were separated only by the depth and width of Geehi. Looking up and up, he felt himself climbing, leading his horse, felt the imagined breathlessness, felt the imagined heat.

He forgot Rickie, forgot everything except the mountains that he would some time climb.

Alex bundled them all back into the Land Rover, and they drove down the great steep Wall to where a big bend seemed hung over the depth of Geehi—where the shining river could be seen, at least six hundred feet below, and the mountains rose almost straight up, beyond.

Only a little lower down the road went right to the edge of the Wall Creek.

'The old cattle track went down the creek from here,' Alex said to Rickie and Margaret, 'down through the tree-ferns. The fronds were like a green roof overhead, and the water ran underfoot. There was always a kind of green gloom, even at high noon,' he went on, 'and bars of sunlight on the red beasts' hides, and you would hear a lyrebird calling like a bell.'

Sally looked at him, half puzzled. Her father and mother seemed to own their memories, and value them, far more than they valued things they could touch, like the car, or tables and chairs.

The journey for the twins was a strange blend of their parents' stories of the mountains, their own memories and the impressions of what they saw now. All their lives they had heard the names of these places —Geehi, Hannel Spur, Groggin, Little Mick, The Leatherbarrel, Dead Horse Gap—and since the coming of the road they had built up their own idea of it all.

There was the great height and depth, and the great white ribbon gums reaching up to the sky; there were the steep spurs like staircases leading upwards; the gentle, safe flats of Groggin, and the waters of the Indi River, lovely for swimming; there was the beautiful forest, changing, as they climbed, from the grey peppermints and brown stringybarks, wattles and bottle-brushes, to candlebarks and ribbon gums, then to the giant mountain ash, and lastly the snowgums; there were the beckoning peaks over the bush—the Pilot, Pinnabar . . . some day they would ride there.

At last Dead Horse Gap was slung across the sky ahead of them—the crescent gap with its cattle yard, its hut invisible in trees, with one ridge stretching up to the Ramshead Range and one towards the Cascades, the mythical home of the brumbies—Dead Horse Gap with the Crackenback Valley beyond.

'There it is!' cried the twins. 'There's Dead Horse Gap!'

'It is!' Their father's voice was as eager as theirs. 'We'll unload, and put on our rucksacks. Then away we go!'

For some unknown reason Sally found herself thinking: 'This is it! Away we go!' and she did not mean just 'away we go across the mountains'. The red bull may have been the first thing the old aborigine had mentioned, but Sally felt sure that now they were starting on something—a search, a chase, the answering of a challenge—she really did not know what.

6 : Moths and brolgas

'Look!' cried Sally. 'You were right. The snowgums are flowering.'

Her mother drove the Land Rover on to the earth beside the road, out of the way of other cars, and stopped it. She swung open her door and got out, with Sally tumbling out behind her. In a moment they were racing each other across the road, jumping up the bank, scrambling up to the trees that surrounded the hut and standing with their faces in among the creamy balls of fluff that covered the snowgums like a pale honey-coloured snowfall.

'We said we'd come when the snowgums were flowering, didn't we?' Her father had joined them and was laughing.

Back at the Land Rover the twins were torn between their desire to climb as high as they could see on to a peak of the Ramshead, and their wish to go towards the Cascades where the wild horses run. Rickie was quite sure that he wanted to go hunting brumbies. While the rucksacks were being sorted the talk about which way they would go was like a mountain breeze blowing this way and that.

'Towards the Cascades, then,' said Alex, who thought the walk to the top of the Ramshead might be too long and that it would be disappointing if they did not reach the top.

Sally and David, followed by the two Adamses, ran headlong down the slope to the heather-covered swamp that was one of the heads of the Crackenback River. The air was cool and scented. Sally felt it flowing through her hair. The snowgrass was so springy on the gentle hillside that she could imagine she had seven-league boots on, as she went leaping down the grey-green slope, with David's long strides matching hers.

They were almost at the swamp, jumping the first little pool of water, knee-high in heather.

'Come down a little further,' said David. 'We'll find a pool clean enough to drink from. Water at the source of the Crackenback should be magic!'

'Gee! You're an awful goat,' said Rickie, just catching up.

David had forgotten Rickie. He leapt gaily from

one heather island to another, then on to a circlet of snowgrass.

'Goat, am I? Never mind: to be a goat is glorious fun.' He threw himself on his face on the grass and cupped his hands in the clear pool. His own face looked back at him from the water, then Sally's face came into the pool too, the same except for the longer hair.

'I keep expecting to see another reflection,' said David. 'We are right at the beginning of a river, which is an exciting place, and I keep thinking that Black Mag might appear. She did say something about understanding being found in the mountains.'

They drank and sprang to their feet, suddenly joining hands and dancing round and round till they fell over, laughing, on the circle of grass.

Margie stood watching them on the slope of the hill beside the swamp, her laughter ringing out with theirs.

'Come on,' said Rickie. 'Let's go and find these brumbies.'

Alex and Joanna had spread a map on the snowgrass and were sitting beside it eating tomatoes.

'We will go up here,' Alex said, pointing with a piece of stick.

'Dead Horse Ridge,' said Rickie.

'Yes, and then along here on to Bob's Ridge. That is where I think there is just a chance of seeing brumbies, in a little snowgrass hollow, like a bowl, hidden by forest and rock ridges. Brumbies used, once upon a time, to be there quite often.'

David took one regretful look up towards the

Ramshead. There were rocky tors on the way up the spur. He noticed a movement on one of them and watched intently. Yes, there it was again, and then, against the blue sky, small and far away, he saw the silhouette of a slim, young aboriginal warrior, pointing his spear towards the south and the Cascades.

He grabbed Sally's arm and pointed. She gasped, but said nothing because of Rickie and Margaret. Then, even as they watched, there was no one on the rocks, and their father was folding up the map. Everybody was getting up off the grass and getting ready to go.

'He was pointing south,' David whispered to Sally. 'We're going the right way,' and they, too, went, striding gaily up the old cattle track on the ridge, taking note of everything: the snow daisies, the trigger plants, the bacon-and-egg shrubs—quite definite in their own minds that they would not see the warrior again, or not for some time.

The scent of the snowgums drifted in waves. The gay piping of birds sounded, and then their chatter.

'Lowrie, lowrie, lowrie-o,' chanted David. 'Out fly the gay red lowries! Red and blue, red and blue.'

'And a robin for us to follow,' said Sally. 'See! He must spend his summer here. We've not seen him since winter-time.'

'The grey thrushes spend summer in the mountain forests, too,' her mother said. 'One flew across the road, down in the mountain ash.'

David swung himself on a snowgum limb and Sally watched the silver bark catching the light as he swung: silver, green and red, the tree moved, the leaves letting through dapples of sunlight. David swung and swung, the tree and the length of his body making, between them, a rhythm.

'I wonder what it is that is going to happen, what it is we must find, what we must do?' he thought, and swung off on to his feet to go along with the others.

Soon they came to a lovely open snowgum wood and then a wide, unbroken field of snowgrass. The children started running through the trees, jumping fallen branches, till the trees ended and they were in the open.

'Race you!' called Rickie.

'Blow it! Here we go!' Joanna murmured under her breath.

Rickie could race them, and he did race them, but, as far as Joanna and Alex could see, the four seemed quite cheerful. Apparently Rickie was not rubbing in his superior speed, the exhibition of his powers being sufficient, but soon David would feel that he had to prove himself also.

Before either of their parents could think of anything to divert them, the twins had sprung up into quite a large snowgum, and were scrambling up the whippy branches like two willy-willies, whirlwinds spiralling upwards.

Rickie was hopelessly outclassed. Joanna sighed. Rickie might be being difficult at present, but she liked him.

The twins were trying to go from branch to branch like possums when Sally seemed to fly out of the tree and pounce on something on the ground.

'A black cockatoo's tail-feather,' she called. 'What luck! It is black with a yellow tip, and perfect.'

The others collected round her.

'It's not quite moulting time yet,' Joanna said, 'so we're hardly likely to find more, but we might as well look,' and they spread out, searching over the snow-grass and cattle pads, while a sparrow-hawk hovered, silver and buff, overhead.

There was more warmth in the sun now, and the scent from the snowgum blossoms came even more strongly. They went on, light-footed, along the top of the ridge, but finding no more feathers. After almost an hour more they were getting close to the brumbies' secret hollow.

'Now we must be as silent as blacktrackers,' Alex told them. 'Follow me!' He struck off the track towards the east.

The twins and Rickie and Margaret all knew how to walk silently. The twins spent quite a lot of time tracking kangaroos in the Tiarri hill paddocks, and had learnt never to crack a twig or rustle leaves as they walked. On snowgrass, of course, it was much easier.

They went along quietly but quite fast, with swinging strides, the twins following their father, then Rickie, and Margaret next, with Joanna behind her. David and Sally were alert, watching for anything and everything. It was always fun to be out in the bush, wondering what you would see, but today was far more exciting than usual. Not only were they watching for any faint movement which might be a wild horse, but they did not want to miss any bird or animal, any wild-flower or shrub. It was as if every part of the bush could hold a message for them. David once saw the beady eye of a young snake, the pointed head and flickering tongue, but it was gone the moment he saw it, so there was no reason to say anything. A kurrawong called in the trees nearby and its call echoed in the nerves of his body. He felt so tense and watchful that he was sure his skin would prickle if a horse was anywhere near. A leaf brushed his bare arm and he jumped. Suddenly he stopped and looked intently at the ground. There on one little patch of wet earth was a hoof-mark!

Joanna was beside him in a second. Ahead, Alex had found another spoor. There was no distinct track to follow, the snowgrass was too thick, but every few yards they found one imprint, or sometimes two.

They hastened along, breathless with excitement, and came near the top of a ridge where the snowgums were thicker. A spine of rocks seemed to be across the top. David was wondering if the brumbies' hollow was beyond when his father half turned and put his finger to his lips. Presently there were rocks underfoot and the rough, strong feel of rocks in their hands. Alex beckoned everyone up, so that they went over the last of the rocks abreast of one another instead of in single file, and not one was the first to see what they saw. Simultaneously, six pairs of eyes peered over the top of the rocks into the hollow below.

David had been asking himself: 'Will it be empty? Will it be empty?' Now they all looked in. He drew in his breath sharply and heard Sally draw in hers too.

There were eight—no, nine—brumbies, six of them grazing peacefully around three young colts who were rearing and playing.

There was a wild screeching, and a flock of jays began to cry their warning to the horses. The three colts paused in their play, two of them in a half-rear. The grazing mares and big, bay stallion threw up their heads, their ears pricked, sniffing the wind. Then suddenly, swiftly, and without even a neigh, they all wheeled and galloped for some hidden opening in the rock wall, their manes and tails flying. In barely ten seconds the last flowing tail had vanished, and below the watchers there was only an empty hollow and a little pool that reflected the bright light of the sun.

For a few seconds they sat in silence, then Rickie spoke:

'What rotten luck those jays spotted us,' he said. 'We might have caught one.'

Sally gave a tremendous sigh and said:

'They looked wonderful.'

All six sat on the rocks looking down into the brumbies' hollow, discussing the horses.

'I'd like to go down there and look around,' David said, and he was hoping that Rickie would not say he was coming too.

'Race you down there,' said Rickie.

'I don't want to race,' said Sally suddenly. 'I want to go quietly in case there is anything interesting to see.'

In the end they all went down.

They stood around the pool. The water caught and held a rainbow-encircled reflection of the sun, and

Sally stood peering into it, wondering what the rainbow meant. Since New Year's Day, and the words spoken by the old aborigine, everything seemed to have some hidden meaning.

Presently they followed the brumby tracks, wherever they showed on the bare earth, all the way to the hidden opening in the rocks, and went through it to look into the swiftly widening valley beyond—and to realize that there was not a sign of a brumby.

As they went back to the hollow David touched Sally on the arm and whispered:

'This is the sort of place there could be a cave. "Dragon-fly Cave" . . . remember?'

Sally nodded, watching Rickie to make sure he had not heard.

Rickie was bending over the last yard of soft earth before the rocks started, looking at the tracks, and was taking no notice of them. Just then Sally saw another, very narrow, opening in the rocks and pulled her twin's arm as she stepped quietly away from the others and slid sideways into it.

At one time this narrow place could have been just a straight passage between two enormous rocks, but then a large piece must have broken off the lower half of the right-hand rock blocking the passage and making a sort of little cave below the overhang. In mid-morning, during midsummer, there was some light in it.

'David!' said Sally sharply. 'Look!'

The rock wall was very smooth where it had been broken, and it was quite possible to make out two reddish drawings on its surface. One was a very large bird with long legs like a brolga, and one quite definitely a moth.

David gasped in amazement.

'A brolga!' he said. 'This must be why he pointed this way.'

'And the moth must be a bogong moth,' said Sally.

'What *luck*!' David whispered, standing with his hands in his rucksack straps. 'But it isn't the Dragon-fly Cave.'

Their father's voice called them from outside.

'No,' Sally agreed, 'it isn't the Dragon-fly Cave, and Black Mag didn't say anything about a brolga cave, only the Brolga Moon. Come on, we must call Mummy and Daddy to come and see it.' She wriggled back into the open, her excitement mounting. 'Mummy! Daddy! Come and see what we've found.'

'Cave?' asked Joanna, raising one eyebrow at her daughter.

'Sort of,' Sally answered.

Joanna slid into the small opening and then suddenly gave a whistle. Alex had come in beside her and now he carefully studied the drawing of the brolga.

'How interesting,' he muttered. 'Have to tell someone at the university or the museum about this.'

'Let's have a look round to see if there are any more,' suggested David.

'Is it really an aboriginal drawing?' asked Rickie who, with Margaret, had arrived last.

'I think so,' Joanna answered. 'It's quite a find.'

'Nice smooth piece of rock for drawing,' said Margaret.

'I expect that is why the drawings are there . . . some aborigines going up for their autumn feed of moths.' Alex nodded. 'Let's look for any others.'

Out of the cool slit in the rocks it seemed as if the day had become warmer. The whole party scrambled hither and thither but no other paintings were found. It became so easy to imagine shapes and shades of colour that they went back to reassure themselves that the moth and the bird did really exist. There they were, faint, but undoubtedly there.

At last Joanna suggested climbing the two or three hundred feet back on to the ridge, finding a creek head, and eating their lunch looking over the Indi Valley to Mount Pinnabar.

★   ★   ★   ★   ★

They found water a little way down the other side of the ridge, and an open snowgrass field on which to lie, with mountain-rice flower bushes, blue asters and snow daisies to make it into a garden. They got water for the billy, collected dry eucalypt sticks and soon had the billy on the fire.

When the billy boiled they ate their lunch slowly and peacefully, and drank billy tea with its unforgettable fragrance of eucalypt smoke, and they lay still for a while and listened to stories which Joanna and Alex told of other days in the mountains.

7 : Lagoon swimming

A FEW DAYS LATER David stood on the end of the long springboard where it was fastened to the bank of the Tiarri swimming lagoon.

'Listen!' he said, holding up a hand. 'He's coming!'

A harsh crying came closer and closer, then, with blue wings and back glittering, a kingfisher flew straight as a piercing sword, straight up the willow-lined lagoon to his favourite dead branches that over-hung the water.

'He's so blue, such a shiny, lacquered blue,' Sally said, 'and I love the silver-white collar and breast. It's

E   65

true that we've never found a kingfisher feather, but I'm sure that is what Black Mag meant by the blue bird.'

'I've got a feeling that unless we find a kingfisher feather we won't get to the cave,' said David.

'It could be another way round,' Sally said. 'Perhaps we must each find a kingfisher feather to bring us luck whenever we are in danger.'

'She talked as if we'd be in danger often,' said David.

Both twins had walked along the board and were balancing at its end, holding on to willow twigs and looking up the lagoon.

'Look, Mother is going to swim quite close to him again,' David whispered. 'He's getting very quiet.'

They watched while Joanna went gliding across the lagoon in a silent breast stroke till she was almost below the bird on his branch. The kingfisher took no notice. When she turned to come back it only started to preen its feathers.

Joanna drew herself out of the water on to the end of the low board and the twins moved back to give her room.

'Do you think if we both went over very quietly he might still stay there?' Sally asked.

Joanna stood dripping, shaking the water out of her hair.

'Try, and see. He doesn't mind us or he wouldn't keep coming back each year. This is the third summer I've known him have his nest here.'

'No, he can't mind us like the snakes do,' laughed David. 'There are less and less of them every year.'

'I'd always look where I stepped, though,' Joanna murmured.

The twins let themselves silently into the water, Sally first, then David.

David, as he swam, was saying to himself:

'Don't move. I can recognize you on a branch from a long way off: I can tell your flight through the air. Let me see you very close, just this once.'

The bird sat on the branch, motionless. Perhaps it watched its own beautiful reflection in the water of its pool. Then it saw the two gliding swimmers, the white heads breaking the surface quietly, and the faces turning up to him. With steady eye, the kingfisher looked at the children, long enough for them to see the gleaming glory of his feathers, and then, with a raucous cry, he flew across to the willow above Joanna's head.

The twins turned over on their backs, watching his flight. Higher up above, a whistling eagle hung in the clear sky.

'Come on in, Mummy,' David called. 'He let us watch him for a little while.'

Joanna dived in and swam out to them. Just then another whistling eagle, perhaps attracted by the splash, flew low over the crescent-shaped lagoon, its fierce head, with hooked beak and cruel eye, peering down at them. Joanna lay on her back, turned her face up to him, and copied his own whistle so that the bird circled even lower and peered more intently. The twins could see his buff markings on his outstretched brown wings, noting, as they had so many times before, how the wing-tips were like fingers spread against the sky.

'He has realized he is being mocked,' laughed David. 'He looks quite disgusted.'

The eagle went then, and was hidden from sight by the willows that surrounded the big curve of water. David shut his eyes, but the after-image of the bird, a smouldering, hovering eagle, was there against the darkness of his eyelids.

Sally and Joanna had pulled themselves up on to the raft and David swam towards them.

Sally was speaking as he pulled himself out of the water.

'I wonder,' she said, 'if our friend the kingfisher will ever spare us a feather?'

'We'll search,' said David. 'Perhaps we'll be lucky this moult or next one.'

'We might as well keep our eyes out for a flash of blue feather any time,' Sally said, 'though the moult hasn't really started. I couldn't bear to have to wait till next year to find out what Black Mag meant.'

Back in the water, Joanna did a swift sprint, thinking how often one had to wait—till much longer than 'next year'. Then she turned over on her back and stretched her arms above her head so that she floated perfectly still on the surface.

Sally watched her, then she, too, rolled over on her back and stretched her arms over her head and floated.

'I wish I had an idea what Black Mag did mean,' she thought. 'And I wonder what the next thing was after the charging red bull?' She floated on and on and the water lapping in her ears seemed to be whispering. Then the memory crept into her mind: 'The next thing was "chasing the mad bullock".'

8 : The mad bullock

BLISTERING SUNSHINE bleached the paddocks, from the Murray Gates to Lake Alexandrina. Under the great Californian redwood trees, outside the Adamses' garden, the shade was deep and cool, but here, scarlet with heat and anger, Rickie and David faced each other.

'What the blazes has got into you?' David's hands were clenched. 'Always trying to beat me, always trying to be the best. You're just too beastly superior.'

'And you're no good. You're hopeless at any games, and you're frightened to fight me because you know I'm better than you!' Rickie's voice was maddening, mocking.

'I know you can beat me,' David fairly spat the words out, 'but take that!' and he aimed a fist for Rickie's nose.

David knew nothing of fighting, but he was angry and moved more quickly than Rickie expected. Rickie dodged only enough for the blow to land on his cheek rather than his nose.

Rickie had had one boxing lesson each week for three school terms. He hit David fair between his eyes and had time to think that he had never seen David glare with fury like that before or his mouth in such a straight line. He ducked below David's open-handed smack, and punched him straight on the mouth.

When David tasted blood in his mouth his hitting became wilder, and the blows that got home on Rickie were more rare. The two boys in blue shirts and faded jodhpurs milled round and round on the slippery pine-needles, and Rickie was giving David about as good a beating as it was possible for a boy of his age to give. Against an immense tree-trunk, Sally and Margaret stood, silent and dismayed, Sally's face becoming very red as she saw her twin get blow after blow.

Margaret found her voice first and began to shout. 'Stop, Rickie! Stop!'

Rickie went on pounding at David.

Suddenly someone came through the trees, and Rickie's father grabbed him by the collar and shook him.

'How dare you behave like this to your visitor! How dare you take an advantage over your old friend! You've had boxing lessons!' Brian Adams looked at David aghast. Bruises and swellings were already beginning to show. 'You little beast,' he said to Rickie, and then looked at his son with pity too. 'I suppose you've taken out on poor David what someone else has given you.' He put an arm round the shoulders of each boy. 'Come on, shake hands,' he said, 'and don't do this to your friends again, Rickie.'

It was almost beyond David to stop himself crying, but he managed to shake hands with Rickie and smile a twisted smile at Sally.

Brian Adams marched them both up to the house for washing and plastering. In the bathroom he started to bathe David's face himself, but sent Margaret to find her mother.

The bathing stung David, and the anointing of the broken skin hurt still more. He wished, bitterly, that he could go riding home, but he and Sally were spending the day with the Adamses, and it would soon be lunch-time. The choking feeling that he was going to cry kept getting worse and worse, and he knew Sally was nearly crying too.

Rickie, who only had the skin broken on one cheek-bone, kept looking at him fiercely, sideways, so that his father might not see, as though saying: 'Go on, howl! You're absolutely licked. I bet you're a cry-baby too!'

Jane Adams, when she was half-way through anointing his face, sent Rickie to her room to wait for her there. Then she finished the job on David.

'Now,' she said. 'You and Sally hop on to your ponies and ride down to the river till lunch-time.' When she was gone, they were out of the door in a second, running towards the stables, David with a ring-ing sound in his ears, and blinding tears in his eyes.

'I'm going to get a drink,' he said, when they reached the river, but even the good water choked him, and he stood up and hooked his arm over Buckwong's neck, shaken by tremendous sobs. Buckwong sniffed at his hair, then the soft nose nuzzled at his battered face.

Sally got off The Banjo, for once at a loss for the right thing to say to her twin. The experience of being beaten was his, and bitter; they were separated by it.

At last they sat down by the river, the two ponies' heads by their shoulders. After a while David found he could swallow the badly needed drink.

Rainbow birds were swooping and diving above the water, green, blue, bronze, perfect and glorious. One caught a dragon-fly in the air, and there was the shimmer of its silver gauze wings in the bird's beak.

'I think Rickie feels we are a bit barmy,' said Sally. 'In fact he says we are mad, getting so much fun watching the birds and things like that. He said you were an ass about the magic in the source of the Crackenback. That's probably what's the matter, and he'd think we were worse than mad if he knew about Black Mag.'

'I'll have to learn how to fight so that I can beat him as soon as possible,' said David, but he was watching the rainbow birds as he spoke.

'Oh, blow it! Then you'd be just as silly as Rickie.'

David laughed, and his cut lips hurt.

'What with old Black Mag and her mutterings of us passing through dangers, and Rickie having me set all the holidays, I'm beginning to feel jumpy.'

'The holidays are nearly over,' said Sally, 'and we've come today to say goodbye to Rickie. . . . Some goodbye!'

David groaned.

'And I'll have to be polite to him all afternoon when we're mustering and picnicking afterwards.'

'Yes, you will, but in a few days he'll go off to school.'

'That's something,' said David, his voice bitter. 'Do you think he feels superior just because he goes to school, and makes other friends, while we do correspondence school work at home?'

'Don't know,' said Sally.

★   ★   ★   ★   ★

Back at the homestead, Jane Adams was talking to Rickie. Inwardly blaming herself that she had not realized that Rickie felt so badly about David, she could see now that she should not have asked the Danes to spend the day, even though the children had always enjoyed being together before this. Jane felt that somehow poor Rickie had not only been paying David for hurts which others had given him, but had been trying to beat something out of David that he envied. Just now she had to try and get the hatred out of Rickie— and hope that the ride to the river had given David a chance to get himself under control again.

She left Rickie smouldering and also nearly in tears, and went off to find Brian.

'It's difficult,' said Brian. 'Can't whack him, really,

and I feel it's partly our fault. Anyway, I'll take them mustering right after lunch.'

'Lunch is going to be a merry meal, isn't it!' said Jane, who was always so busy at meal-times, coping with children and food. With relief, she saw the twins coming back. She had half thought they might go home!

David carried himself very straight as he walked towards the house. He was ashamed of himself for taking such a beating, but he also knew that Rickie's fierceness was unfair, and that the attack had been unfair too. He wished most dreadfully that he did not have to stay. Everyone would be feeling awkward.

When they went to wash their hands he saw his face in the mirror—the knuckle-marks, the black eye and the swollen lips—and he saw it redden with misery. There was no disguising the fact that he had taken a real beating. If *only* he could go home.

Mrs. Adams, guessing that it would be difficult for David to join the others without appearing self-conscious, met the twins in the corridor and took them into the dining-room.

The children had been told that they must not speak about David's face, but nothing could stop them looking at the exciting sight which he presented and which every moment was getting worse as the bruises darkened.

Rickie looked with interest at his handiwork and began to feel a little guilty. Everyone who saw that face would know the fight had not been in fun. They would also know that he could fight, but he was beginning to wonder how proud of himself he should be.

Margaret asked if she could sit next to David. Jane and Brian Adams tried to keep up the conversation. Even David noticed how the usually silent 'Uncle Brian' was doing everything he could to help him through an awkward meal. To make everything worse, his mouth would not open properly for him to put in the food which he did not want, and every attempt hurt him. It seemed to him that Rickie was maliciously watching his efforts to make his mouth work. Even dear, fat little Elizabeth was watching him.

At last the meal was over and Brian gathered them all up to go mustering. David gladly walked out of the house to the stables and got on to Buckwong, feeling a different person once he was astride his pony.

The mustering which was to be done was not difficult. The remainder of a mob of bullocks, out of which the fats had gone to market that morning, had to be rounded up in a fairly small paddock and brought along past the house to a river paddock lower down.

Everything was sleepy. Sleepy cattle blundered slowly out from beneath the trees where sleepy magpies warbled their hot-day song. David rode through the redgums and the scrub bushes, pushing the unwilling red beasts out of their camping places, sitting straight and easily in the saddle, half conscious that this was his element, wishing the morning had never happened.

More cattle lay under a group of redgums, two beasts were standing between the great, knotted trunks. He noted with surprise that one of these was more like a store bullock, without any condition on it. The others were all fat, just going to a better paddock to be topped off for market. The store bullock set off at a thundering gallop, his head down, dust flying from his hooves. David frowned, hoping the fats would not gallop—he had no wish to make Brian Adams angry—but the heavy beasts lumbered out into the sun at their own slow pace.

The mob was beginning to collect: the riders were getting closer together. Buckwong pricked his ears, seeing the other horses. David bent and caressed the pony's black mane and withers.

The Banjo and Sally came into view, and Buckwong, knowing he was in a strange place, and he and The Banjo the strangers, threw up his head and neighed. David pressed lightly with his legs and Buckwong broke into a canter towards his stable-mate.

From time to time, as the mob collected, David noticed the rangy store bullock. It was always bucking, or horning, or galloping head down, always causing a little trouble with the others, or just an uneasiness among the nearest fats. Once it broke from the bullocks that he and Sally were driving in front of them, and he galloped after it and swung it back. His head ached when he moved fast.

When the whole paddock was mustered, they drove the cattle towards the gate—all the musterers together for the first time since they had started. Mr. Adams went round the mob to open the gate and count them through.

David turned to Sally.

'I guess Uncle Brian will notice that store beast while he's counting them,' he said.

The children followed through the gate when the last beast was through.

'Shut the gate, Rickie,' his father said, and added: 'We've got one beast too many.'

'Did you see the rather nervous store bullock?' David asked shyly, because it would not do to appear more observant than either Rickie or his father. 'I brought him over from the big patch of redgums.'

'Didn't see him,' Mr. Adams said, looking puzzled, 'not even when I was counting.'

They drove the mob over the creek and along the track towards the homestead. The rangy bullock was in the centre of the mob. There were only about fifty beasts, so it was easy to keep an eye on him. After a while David noticed he was making his way towards the lead, on the side where he was riding.

The track broadened out into quite a road and went round the homestead garden fence. Brian Adams was on the outside wing, and David was urging them quietly along the fence. Suddenly he noticed Elizabeth at a gate watching them, golden hair shining.

The store bullock had moved to the edge of the mob and it saw her. It stopped and snorted. Elizabeth gave a little scream and turned and ran.

David, knowing one should never run like that from a bullock, exclaimed in sudden fear, as the beast broke into a lumbering canter straight for the gate.

David pushed Buckwong into a gallop, but the bullock had crashed through the top rail before he could head him. He saw Elizabeth running on her short, fat legs, then he saw the splintered gate coming towards him. Even with the top rail gone, it was higher than anything he had ever jumped.

'Up, Buckwong, up!' he gasped, urging the pony with hand, leg and voice. But Buckwong needed no urging. He flew the broken gate and was after the beast in a second.

David heard someone shouting and realized that Mrs. Adams was running at the beast from one side. The bullock apparently heard her and checked for a moment. In that one moment he brought his whip down across its face.

Suddenly Sally and Brian Adams were beside him. Jane Adams had scooped up Elizabeth and put her in safety with the baby on the high verandah, and was coming back, armed with a garden stake. The blinding excitement was nearly over.

'Open the gate, or what's left of it, Sal,' Mr. Adams said, 'then come back and help us drive him through.'

Outside, Rickie and Margie were holding the mob, but the leaders could be seen between the garden trees further down the track. The bullock, after looking wildly at the three riders and at Mrs. Adams, galloped towards the leaders, oblivious of the fence or of flower-beds and flowering shrubs.

'This,' thought David, 'is really Uncle Brian's job. There's going to be damage done in the garden.' He cantered Buckwong carefully down a path, watching the bullock crash the fence and recoil as the rail and wire netting held fast. Then Brian Adams got in behind it with his heavy whip, and the bullock, trampling and destroying, went towards the gate.

David and Sally rode out behind him, David still feeling the strange hollow of fear in his stomach. He was surprised when Rickie, with unbelievable generosity, rode up to him and said:

'You did well to jump that gate and follow the bullock.'

'He did more than "well",' his father said, his voice rather sharp.

Sally, who, having seen it all, knew that David had been swift and brave, heard the sharpness in Mr. Adams's voice and realized that perhaps it was awkward to have David risk his own neck to save Elizabeth when Rickie had smashed him up so much that morning. For the first time since the boys' fight her face relaxed into a delighted grin.

The paddock where they were leaving the cattle was one through which the twins would have to pass on their way home. David, as he watched the red and white backs in front of him, was wondering if he could think of any good reason for going on back to Tiarri, but however much he wished he was riding along the track by the river, he knew that to leave now would only give Rickie another chance to jeer.

Jane Adams had already telephoned Joanna telling her to expect her son to have a battered face, and when the musterers got back Joanna and Alex had come over for the picnic.

David took a deep breath as he saw them, but Sally, desperate that no one should ask about his face, cantered

up to the group and excitedly told their mother and
father how he had jumped Buckwong over four bars
of the gate when the bullock was after Elizabeth.

David could not believe that anything could out-
weigh the morning's disgrace. His eyes met his mother's.
By no flicker of expression did she show that she had
seen the marks that told of his beating. Her smile was
the whole-hearted smile he wanted. Then, with his
head up, he went on with the other children to tie up
their ponies in the shade.

Once he had lived through this afternoon, something very unpleasant would be over. He must swim
with the others, and race, and play on the banks, however much it hurt, and try to eat enough at the picnic
tea to stop anyone being aware that he still felt sick.

It was while he was standing on the bank beside
Sally, in the dappled light and shade of a willow, that
he suddenly seemed to hear a voice and see a picture
in his mind of the galloping bullock. The picture and
the voice fitted together like a puzzle that had come
right.

He turned to Sally.

'That was the mad bullock,' he said, his voice
excited. 'Remember? "In front of the charging red
bull, chasing the mad bullock"?'

'Why, yes. You must be right.' Then she looked at
him with the impish grin that she had worn since he
had chased the bullock. 'Funny she didn't say anything
about the fists of your friend and neighbour.'

'Yes, she might have warned me, mightn't she?'

9 : The striking snake

'THE THING TO DO,' said David, as they sorted their books for school work, 'is to find a kingfisher feather. Somehow I'm sure that "the feather of the blue bird, dropped as it flies" would bring us luck if we are really going to meet all the dangers that the old woman mentioned.'

'We'll really have to go searching for one.' Sally looked for her pen.

'We'll start this afternoon,' said David. 'Daddy has visitors, so there'll be no cattle or sheep work to do.'

'And we'll go to any kingfisher haunt that we

know,' said Sally eagerly. 'It will be a lovely afternoon. We can count how many interesting birds we see in the one afternoon.'

In the garden the hot sun burnt through clear, dry air. The mauve daisies were starting to flower and already the pink, and blue, and white hydrangeas that had heralded Christmas were turning deep red and green. It was almost the end of February. David's face had healed, and for two weeks there had been nothing to disturb life's usual rhythm. Just summer slowly turning to autumn. Even though there had been no strangeness in any of the happenings of the last two weeks—nothing that seemed suddenly to fulfil the words spoken by the old lubra, down there where the two streams meet—the twins had talked about her a lot, and wondered 'what next?'.

They were supposed to be settled down to school work, but until their mother came, some minutes later, the arithmetic was punctuated by odd sentences about kingfishers, and feathers, and birds. One of their great interests for years had been the birds that lived around their valley or the ones that came and went every year.

Their mother arrived and work had to be given more attention. The morning grew warmer and warmer.

The school work came on the mail every fortnight, and had to be done and then sent to the teacher in Melbourne for correction. Sometimes it was difficult to appreciate the importance of arithmetic when there was mustering to be done, or harvesting, or shearing.

*   *   *   *   *

Joanna wiped the perspiration off her top lip.

'Long division is a bit of a pill, but, as Samuel Whiskers would say, "I am persuaded that it is necessary".'

'He said "indigestible",' murmured David. 'He was speaking about knots, but I am persuaded he was right about this sum too.'

'I'll race you both to the answer,' his mother laughed, 'and then we'll get a drink. It's the last sum, isn't it?'

'Hooray!' said Sally.

'Don't get too gleeful, there's a whale of a lot of grammar too,' David groaned.

'There's some interesting geography and science in this parcel of work,' Joanna said. 'We're to do plasticine relief maps of Australia, and two different projects are suggested: either drawings of trees, leaves and fruits, or drawings of three different birds and written notes on their habits.'

The twins looked up, interested.

'Birds for us!' Sally said. 'But we could do lots more than three.'

'We'll get some fun out of this,' David's face was bright, 'but I wonder how much we really know about them?'

Joanna picked up her pencil.

'You can say when they arrive, when they go, what they do while they are here, where they nest, what they eat, what their call is like. Also you know such things as when you hear gang-gangs there's often rough weather coming to the mountains.'

Sally nodded.

'M'm. Same applies to kurrawongs in summer, and of course black cockatoos.'

Joanna pulled the paper towards her.

'Come on, the last sum,' she said, 'then grammar and reading.'

Joanna finished her sum first. Usually she did the day's arithmetic the night before, now that it had become really difficult, but last night there had been so many figures in the office work, the cost of fencing and suchlike to be worked out, that she had gone to bed too tired to do any more. Now she sat looking out into the garden, thinking that autumn was nearly coming and that they must go to the mountains again. There was always so much to do that some of the pure delights of living had to be put off. The local agricultural show was fairly soon, too, she reflected.

The sums were finished, and not one answer tallied with another! Line by line they checked, till the mistakes were corrected and the answer found. They got themselves drinks and fruit, and Joanna heard the spelling that had been learnt the day before. As she pointed out the sentence to be parsed, and watched the twins start to write it, she heard, with half her attention, a grating cry from high up in the nearest tree.

'Dollar bird,' muttered David, and went on writing.

The dollar bird gave his cackling, grating cry again, and took off to fly through the bright sky. Perhaps he would go to the willows above the lagoon, thought Sally, but, never mind, they would be there themselves when the morning's work was finished.

'I'll be moving the hoses around the garden,' Joanna said. 'If you're not certain about what you're doing, ask me. Don't go on and on doing it wrong.' She walked down the steps.

'Is "lobster" a proper noun or a common noun?' asked Sally.

'Don't know,' said David, and they went on working in silence and with great concentration. They had at last learnt that if they did not work they would be made to stay behind to finish while their mother went out. Only occasionally now did they become stupid on purpose and sit idling till Joanna got completely exasperated, and the ponies were banned for the day and everyone was cross and miserable. But school work was something that simply had to be done.

'You must learn,' Joanna had been saying for years. 'The world becomes more and more enthralling as you seek to understand it.' And as the two disbelieving children had reluctantly learnt the sounds of the letters, put the first few words together, and made small sentences that seemed to them to have no value, she had said it over and over again: 'Reading is the key to a magic world.' Suddenly, one day, this was true.

The telephone rang as Joanna walked up the steps, and she went into the house to answer it. When she came back the grammar was finished, ready to be checked, and the twins were writing out and learning their spelling.

Joanna pulled a book towards her and browsed through the poems.

'See if you like this,' she said.

> 'The song is gone; the dance
> is secret with the dancers in the earth,
> the ritual useless, and the tribal story
> lost in an alien tale.
>
> Only the grass stands up
> to mark the dancing ring: the applegums
> posture and mime a past corroboree,
> murmur a broken chant.'

'Read it again, please, Mummy,' said Sally.

Joanna read it again, her voice quiet in the stillness of the hot morning.

'They're applegums, aren't they, near the gate?' David asked.

Joanna nodded.

'And in the basin below Wattle Gully.'

' "Posture and mime a past corroboree",' Sally said thoughtfully, and Joanna remembered the enrichment that poem had brought to her own life, how those applegums by the gate, under which she so often drove sheep, had acquired a new significance . . . 'posture and mime'. . . .

She turned the pages of Judith Wright's poems and came to 'Trapped Dingo': there was that unforgettable line . . . 'and the white shorn mobs of stars on the hills of the sky . . .' but *she* had heard a dingo howling in the dark ranges and the twins had not. She went on through the book till she found 'Bullocky'. Those words might light up their own experience with a blazing light.

> 'While past the camp fire's crimson ring
> the star-struck darkness cupped him round,
> and centuries of cattlebells
> rang with their sweet uneasy sound.'

School work, if she succeeded in making it seem part of their life, need not be such a grind for the twins, but it was not always easy for them to see the necessity for it when all the rest of life was so interesting.

★   ★   ★   ★   ★

In the afternoon they gave Joanna clear details of where they were going, which was to all the kingfisher haunts they knew.

'Get back by five,' Joanna said, 'and if you are off your ponies do look out for snakes.' Then they rode down the hill towards the river.

'We nearly always see interesting things near the deep pool down the river,' David said. 'There are sure to be ducks, and perhaps swans, blue cranes, spoonbills, anything at all, even a snipe.'

'Even, possibly, a kingfisher,' said Sally, watching a pink and grey cloud of galahs leave a solitary redgum in the horse paddock.

'Look, Sal! Look!' exclaimed David. 'Today is going to be quite a day, I'm sure!'

'What do you mean?'

'Well, we're in luck.'

'Oh,' she said. 'So we are! There are the brolgas.'

David watched them thoughtfully. 'Look how fiery red their heads are, and how warm the grey colour of their feathers is.'

'It's a grey with the faintest pink in it. The blue cranes are blue-grey. It's funny how at this time of year the brolgas come in here and the rest of the time they are either down below or on the other side of the hill.'

'Perhaps they eat grasshoppers,' David said, watching them still. 'Jackie says it's a sign of big rain if they circle very high. Do you remember the four of them high above the house, quite a while ago now? That was before the tornado.'

'Yes, there was a huge halo round the sun that day.' Sally felt herself tense with excitement when she thought of the twisting wind and the beating rain, the hail, the flying branches, the wet wistaria leaves plastered to the windows.

They let themselves out of the horse paddock gate and, once down on the flats, put their ponies into a canter. A little further along they stopped and did some trotting and cantering in circles, and a figure of eight because they thought of the show coming soon. As they drew near to the river they went more quietly. Here they might, indeed, see any sort of bird, or even a platypus. There was a reed bed by shallow, weedy water, and some deep still water to one side of the singing river. Here they had once even seen a seagull riding the Murray as though it were the ocean, and they had wondered ever since where it had come from. Had it come over the mountains from Twofold Bay?

'What are we going to see?' thought Sally. 'It is so exciting watching for everything. What will it be? A spoonbill, or seven blue cranes?' There was a flotilla of nine black swans, gracefully floating on the river.

The twins rode out to a little point, hoping the swans might take off. They pulled up in the shade of a tree, and sat talking, watching the suspicious birds, then they rode a little further towards them and saw them run along the water, beating up a cloud of spray with their wings, then fly downriver into the path of the sun, necks outstretched, red beaks pointing straight to the bright horizon, and Sally had that strange feeling she had had before when she had seen them flying to the sunset, or heard them taking off during a dark winter night, that there was something lost about them, as though they were seeking something they would never find.

As they turned their ponies back, a bird flew straight out from the bank by the still water, almost from under where they had been sitting talking—straight across the river.

'Snipe!' said David, 'and the jolly bird must have been sitting there, listening to us!'

They jumped off their ponies and went to look. Beneath an overhanging rock and some rushes there was a little mound of earth, well trodden, well sprinkled with bird droppings and surrounded by small, creamy, brown-barred feathers.

'Well, I'm blowed!' David said. 'He must sit here often and have a good scratch!'

'We'll come again and bring Mummy,' Sally laughed. 'We'll sneak up on him next time. How funny! He must just sit and look at the deep pool and watch the fairy martens play above the water.'

'I told you we were going to have a good day today, Sal!' David grinned.

A little way up the river there were four or five tall-trunked redgums standing in a curve round a lagoon. These were beloved by dollar birds and whistling eagles; they were also the home of a pair of kingfishers.

Ibis flew up as the children rode along—long lines of white birds forming into signs or letters, spelling out a secret or making an arrow to point the way to treasure or mystery.

Through the air came the sweet cadence of a white-throated warbler from high up a willow. David raised his face towards the sound, feeling suddenly exultant.

'How lovely it all is,' he thought. 'Sally and I know where kingfishers live in summer, where the plovers dance in May. We know where the brolgas like to be. We know the haunts of water rats, and the hollow limbs where possums make their houses. We'll know where the swans build their great floating nests of reeds in the spring, and perhaps we'll see a wild duck's brood.'

Then he wondered if they would ever find a kingfisher feather, because, like a planted seed, the idea had grown in their minds that a kingfisher's feather was absolutely necessary to bring them luck and protect them from danger.

They rode back and forth and round about beneath the tall redgums, searching for a flash of blue. There were tussocks and thick bracken fronds around the foot of the trees, but the sight of a tiger-snake's vanishing coils did not make them want to fossick about on foot. Even the ponies got bored of going backwards and forwards in the same place. After a long time of searching, with eyes never leaving the ground, David looked up and saw the kingfisher. He had flown to his favourite tree, and was sitting up there watching them.

Sally began to laugh.

'Hullo there!' she said, waving her hand to the kingfisher.

'I think,' said David, 'it's time we moved on. I don't think he's going to part with one feather.'

'Goodbye,' called Sally, still laughing. 'Perhaps you'll give us one yet.'

'We'll go to the main runner in the Loop Paddock now, but we won't ride over the bridge,' David laughed, and away they went at a canter, watched by the swift, bright eye of the kingfisher.

'Let's gallop,' called Sally, shortening her reins and leaning forward on The Banjo's neck. Then the wind was racing through her hair, the dark grey pony moving swiftly beneath her.

At the gate she slid off to open it and let the ponies through. They walked more soberly across the next paddock towards the runner. Somehow, now, they did not expect to find a feather. There had been no sign of one under the trees where the kingfisher sat, and though they knew that kingfishers haunted the bends of the runner, they did not know on which trees they sat. So they watched for a flashing blue bird on the wing or a kingfisher shape on a branch.

There were ibis feeding near the runner: there was a nankeen crane sitting on a jutting root, immobile, gazing at the water: there were kookaburras in the willows, little wrens flitting hither and thither. A whistling eagle was eating a rabbit. Willie wagtails chattered as they hovered over the tussocks, and by the river the rainbow birds swept up into the bright sky. There were no kingfishers.

'Our luck is not going to stay with us,' said David, sounding quite cheerful about it.

'Well, we've been too lucky already,' Sally answered, 'and I don't know, but perhaps I love rainbow birds as much as any other bird. They are just not as rare. . . .'

They sat on their ponies watching the birds till David suddenly said:

'We *must* find a kingfisher feather, though, because I've a strong feeling we'll need it.'

Shadows were beginning to lengthen when they turned their ponies towards home, and as they reached the bottom of the hill the sunlight seemed to dance like a flame on the ridge. A stream, lined with willows, flowed at the foot of the hill. Suddenly flashing about the water, blue, rosy pink, haloed by the oblique sunrays, went a pair of azure kingfishers, there for a few seconds and then gone into the willows.

'Oh,' said David, and Sally echoed: 'Oh.'

They rode quietly round the tree where the king-fishers had vanished, and stopped, sitting in silence to search every branch. But there was nothing to be seen, so they rode on, and though they searched all the time, not once more did they see the kingfishers again.

It was as they turned back that the bar of sunlight fell slanting on to a pool and on to a flash of blue that lay caught in the reeds in the heart of the pool.

They both drew a deep breath and said: 'Look!' simultaneously.

They dismounted and walked towards the edge of the water, through the bar of dusty light, and looked at the blue feather shining.

'Easier to get it from the other side, without getting wet,' Sally said.

They dropped their reins on to the ground and walked round the pool. David stepped cautiously out on to a tussock, but it was still too far to step right across to the reeds.

'Here's a stick,' said Sally. 'You might be able to pull the reeds this way and reach it.'

'I'll use it to help me jump to that tussock and then back to the reeds,' David answered, then he heard Sally give a little gasp, and saw, rearing out of the tussock beside them, the flattened head of a tiger-snake—saw the flickering red tongue, the evil, glittering eye.

Quickly Sally brought the stick down, beating the striking neck sideways on to the ground.

'Again!' cried David, as she thrashed and beat at

the twisting coils. 'The ground underneath him is too soft.'

The head came up again and a great curve of snake behind it. The scales were yellow and brown—shining. Sally missed him and he was darting towards her. Down came the stick again and this time she felt a more solid impact, the stick on the flesh, and the flesh on firmer ground. The snake writhed wildly but did not come towards her. Over and over again she hit it.

'He's done!' she gasped, and suddenly saw her hand shaking.

David took the stick from her, slid it under the flexing body, lifted it and threw it far out into the water.

'I think we need that feather,' he said, 'but . . .'

'Try to get it with the stick.'

Sally held on to him while he leant across the still pool and its gold-lit water. Slowly he pulled the reeds with the feather towards him till they could just reach it.

Sally took the feather from his hand.

'Blue as blue,' she said, 'when the light shines on it. We have the feather. David! It was guarded by the "striking snake"!'

'Gee!' said David. 'Of course! I wonder what on earth is going to happen to us in the end? We've had a close go with the bull, and really the mad bullock was only fun afterwards, and now you've been jolly nearly bitten by a tiger-snake!'

'Well, we've got the feather now,' said Sally.

10 : 'A fiver on the little girl'

DAVID leant his shoulder against Buckwong's.

'Move over,' he said, and went on brushing vigorously at the black coat that shone, and gleamed, and glowed.

A few yards further up the fence The Banjo stood, lulled to a state of bliss by Sally's soft singing and the sweep, sweep of the body brush on his neck and shoulders. Only his tail moved to chase away the persistent flies.

David went into the cool gloom of the tack room for a comb. Immediately he was enfolded in the lovely stable smell. Stirrups jingled together as his shoulder bumped them when he passed under the saddle-racks.

'Tar for the hooves,' he thought, then, hearing the trill of rainbow birds, went out into the sunshine to see them, with nothing but the comb in his hand. The rainbow birds were flying in big flocks now, and would soon be going north, away from the approaching winter. He could not bear to miss seeing them whenever he heard their call, and he saw them now, bronze-winged against the sun, green, blue, yellow, all the glory of summer—and they would go.

'Why does this lovely summer have to end?' Sally asked suddenly, for she had been watching the birds too, and sharing David's thoughts.

'It *has* been a lovely summer,' David said, and added rather wistfully: 'There's a lot of swimming weather left yet, and, you know, I think that mountain road is going to be better this winter and we may get much more ski-ing which will make the winter quite different.'

'Yes,' Sally agreed, then she surprised him by saying: 'Do you really want to ride in the show?'

'I don't much mind,' David confessed.

Sally stood back to admire The Banjo.

'I do want to, and Banjo looks so beautiful. But truthfully,' she added, in an effort of great honesty, 'Buckwong looks even more like a show horse.'

Buckwong and Banjo were both galloway height, though lightly built, which meant that the twins would not be competing in the children's classes.

'I don't think Mummy and Daddy are keen on us

riding,' David went on. 'Mummy said that we don't know how the ponies will behave in the ring with all the noise. *I* think they'll be all right.'

'They think we aren't big enough to ride galloways in a show, but it should be great fun. The Gilliats ride their ponies in lots of shows, and have won a good many ribbons.' Sally's voice sounded a little envious. 'They say that most of the judges tell you your faults and how to do better, so that you learn a lot.'

'It was fun when we used to take it in turns riding Glory in the young children's classes,' David said.

Sally gave a cheerful toss of her head so that her old straw hat slid right back.

'It'd be more fun in the real thing. Oh well, maybe they'll decide to let us. Come on, let's mix some feed for these two.'

Together they went into the feed-room and soon the chaff was running through their fingers, making them sneeze with its dry musty smell, and then there was the softness of bran in their hands. They blinked as they walked out into the brilliant sunshine, and heard the low whinnies from the waiting ponies.

Sally saw The Banjo turn his grey head towards her, the nostrils quivering softly. She poured the chaff and bran into The Banjo's box and buried her face in his mane, smelling the lovely, friendly smell of horse.

*   *   *   *   *

Joanna and Alex Dane had gone to the local show year after year. Joanna could remember her father,

G

another blond David Dane, riding a great, rearing black gelding. Now it would be young David looking small and startlingly blond on a black horse. The show-ring would look the same, only the animals and the people would have changed since that day twenty-five years ago, and among the people would still be many old friends who would remember every show and every season for years back.

There was a lot of work in making a good show, and a great deal of organization by the committee and the secretary—yet it had the effect of growing, like a paddock of rye grass, simply out of the life of the district. There might be fights over the cut-flower section, and misery about a feather-light sponge cake that did not get a prize—Joanna had heard acrimonious remarks concerning the judges of a bale of meadow hay, and Alex remembered wild words about the judging of horses and beasts, and about the quality of neighbours' stock, all spoken with such fury that they had a thunderous rhythm—but the day of the show was the happiest day of the district.

The twins woke early, very excited, the morning of the show, knowing that they were to ride in some events, if not all that they could enter, depending on the behaviour of the ponies. The dawn was barely lighting the sky when they looked out of the windows, up the valley to the Alps.

'It's rather hot,' said David. 'It would be a jolly shame if it rained.'

The light crept over a cloudless, but heavy, sky.

'May turn thundery later,' Joanna said at breakfast-time, 'but it's lovely now.' She, too, was dressed in riding clothes and looked a little unusual in a tie instead of open-necked shirt. Alex and Jackie had left an hour ago, to take the horses slowly in to the show-ground.

The twins' excitement rose higher and higher as they helped wash up the breakfast dishes then pack the lunch. Several times they checked over the saddlery and grooming kit that was already in the Land Rover. They gave their elastic-sided riding-boots a final polish—then it was time to go. In David's pocket was a small leather case in which they had put the kingfisher feather.

'May bring us luck,' he had said. 'We'll take it in turns to carry it in our events.'

Now that it was Show Day, David was more excited at the thought of riding than Sally was, more determined that nothing should stop him from com-peting in every possible event. As he held the door open for old Jackie's wife, Dolly, to get into the Land Rover, he touched the canvas roof, smelt the smell of dust, and could already imagine the dust rising all round the side shows and the merry-go-rounds, even in the ring, imagine all the noise and the voice on the microphone calling in the galloway hacks.

He closed the door on Dolly, having carefully helped her in with her best dress, and climbed into the back himself, beside the saddles. Then they were away.

As they reached the showground they pulled up at the ramp to pay the gatekeeper, and David noticed a big white thunderhead cloud framing the pine trees and the grandstand.

Joanna had already seen the thunderheads sailing up over the hills, and thought that most of the day would be over before any storm came. It was not the weather that kept a little nagging anxiety shooting up into her mind, it was something to do with that image of her father on his spirited show horse and of David on the black galloway. Every time she thought of David riding into the ring and saw him in her mind's eye she felt as if something were going to happen.

She drove the Land Rover towards the pine trees where Alex and Jackie had already hitched up the horses. The twins put on cotton smocks over their clean riding clothes, and immediately set to work to groom and polish their ponies again.

At last, when they felt that the ponies were gleaming as much as they could possibly make them, they saddled up and mounted. Joanna and Alex came with them to ride around the ring, and let The Banjo and Buckwong get used to the strange sights and sounds, and all the other horses that were practising figures of eight, or cavorting around.

Already the mares suitable for breeding hacks and hunters were being judged, and in another ring pony stallions were being led round. Amongst the other riders who were giving their horses a try-out, David saw the Gilliats. He also saw a boy of his own age on a beautiful bay pony.

The Adams family had brought a pony for Elizabeth. There were quite a few small children running about in jodhpurs and shirts and velvet caps, pulling Shetlands or other small ponies behind them. A blare of music started up from the merry-go-round. Buckwong stood on his hind legs. The Banjo jumped and trembled a little.

Sally saw David sitting confidently and straight, his seat like the seats of all the riders in Colonel Wynmallen's book, his hands quiet on the reins, his legs, his heels, his toes, all correct, and suddenly she knew that she felt as if she looked like that too. Then rather sadly she thought to herself that even if they were quite good stock riders it did not mean that they would win prizes in a show. For one thing, perhaps they rode a shade too long in the stirrups, and there was a girl, not much older than herself, in a smart riding habit. Good clothes did make you look neater.

'Suppose you canter out and back, and then do a figure of eight,' their father suggested. 'Your first event must be very soon.'

When the galloway classes started they saw that they were the only children riding in them. Sally found that she was trembling so much with excitement that she felt as though her thighs would not grip the saddle. She had the kingfisher feather in her pocket for this event, but it did not give her much confidence.

There were only four other competitors, all adults, two from the district and two visitors from other country centres who were doing a round of the autumn shows on very well-groomed and well-fed professional show ponies.

Sally felt her legs shaking and her hands shaking,

even her lips seemed to quiver. The judge looked enormous and stern. Just then The Banjo turned his dear, grey nose and nuzzled her foot.

She bent down.

'Oh, Banjo darling,' she whispered, and as she sat up she saw one of the local riders, Arthur Wilton, grin at her and beckon her up beside him.

'You and David follow me,' he suggested. 'Those ponies of yours are beauties, but they've not been shown before, and we've got hot competition.' He nodded towards the visiting horses.

David and Sally rode up close to him, and when the judge told them to trot round in a circle they followed behind him.

'Canter!' the judge called, and Sally suddenly found that her trembling had stopped, her lips were smiling, and she and The Banjo moved smoothly together, just as they always did.

A little dust rose from the dry ground. The judge looked hot. Sally had forgotten the crowds, and somehow she no longer heard the noise of engines and blaring, organ-grinder tunes. It was wonderful fun to see what she and The Banjo could do together.

The judge told them to stop and they lined up in front of him. Sally had time to look at David then. He did not appear to be perfectly happy, but he was riding well, and Buckwong looked beautiful.

They were being sent out, one by one, to do a figure of eight. Mr. Wilton gave Sally a grin as he went ahead of her, and a faint, encouraging wink when her turn came. Out she cantered, alone into the ring that seemed to get bigger and bigger as she went. She could hardly make up her mind when or where to make The Banjo change legs and go in the other direction. She checked him, and felt sure her aid was not decided enough and that The Banjo would not know what she meant. For one horrible second the pony seemed to be uncertain, then it changed legs and finished the figure.

David went off looking much more confident than she had, but Sally knew that the almost proud look was the one that David wore when he was summoning up most courage. She could feel each of her twin's movements in her own body, as though she, too, were riding out there. She felt the faint contraction of his thigh muscles as he sat easily to the canter, then the 'feel' of the horse's mouth, the pressure of the near leg.

Buckwong made a perfect figure of eight, and David came back towards her, his face rather pink. Sally could tell, though it was not noticeable for all to see, that Buckwong was jumpy. She knew that the sensation of his nervousness was going up through David's legs, through his hands, right through his whole body—and that David was unable to keep calm and quieten the pony.

The judge came walking round each pony. He ran his hands down their legs, looked at their mouths, stood back and studied them. Sally and David both knew that there was no doubt that the two visiting galloways would get the prizes but they could not help wishing and wishing that somehow the judge would come towards them with the ribbons, and they could not help feeling a shiver of disappointment as the ring steward put the blue and the red ribbons round the visitors' necks.

Sally sat there smiling at the winners, as she had been taught to do, and hoping she did not look disappointed. Her right hand strayed in Banjo's mane and rubbed his wither. Suddenly she realized that the big judge was standing between her and David, patting Banjo and one arm resting on Buckwong.

'Well, young lady,' he said with a wide smile. 'These are nice horses. You've never shown them before. . . . Now, in the "District Galloway", press them more on to the bit, hold your reins a shade tighter and make up your minds very definitely when you mean them to change legs.' He smiled again and moved off. Neither of the twins heard him mutter to his companion: 'Can't give one twin's pony a prize and not the other's.'

This same problem had bothered Joanna a good deal, though after all it was the ponies who were being judged, dissimilar ponies, not the extremely similar twins. However, in the 'District Galloway' the judge solved the problem by tying a red ribbon on each pony's neck, and Joanna and Alex, standing on the edge of the ring, saw the twins' faces lighten with tremendous pleasure.

They did not have another event to ride in for about half an hour, so, leaving their parents to hold the ponies and watch the children under seven riding, the twins set off for ice creams and to see the side shows.

They ducked under the white railings just near the stand and went towards the merry-go-round. Now it *was* hot, and not a puff of breeze went through the crowds.

'Hullo there, twins!' Friendly voices greeted them as they walked side by side. They did not realize that the smiles they saw on faces were not just for friendliness, but for the striking fact of their likeness.

There was Jess, the Adamses' cook and Dolly's sister, in her best dress and shoes. They hurried towards her.

'Jess! Jess!' they called together, in case she got lost in the crowd.

'Well, I declare! If you haven't even grown since the day the bullock went for our fat little Elizabeth. . . . Well, wouldn't that take a rise out of you!' Jess beamed at them both as they kissed her. The twins were what Jess called a real thoroughbred pair and as pleasant to look upon as a yearling colt and filly.

'Those are fine, upstanding horses you're riding,' she said. 'An' they've both got a prize. Now that judge, he knows a horse when he sees one.' Then she hustled them off to buy ice creams and to go to see her prize-winning cake. Finally they reached the merry-go-round, bought their tickets and sat themselves on two wooden horses on the outside so that they would swing the greatest distance. The Gilliat children came into sight. David called them, and the merry-go-round was held back till they had flung themselves on to horses too.

'Away we go!' cried Sally, as the cracked tune started up and they began to go round, slowly at first, then faster, swinging out towards the crowd at the coconut shy.

'Rusty, Rusty!' called David, as he saw a little red-headed man walking away from the snake-pit.

'Hullo, David! Having fun?'

'Wonderful fun,' called David, as they went round and round.

'Wonderful fun . . . wonderful fun,' all the voices seemed to be saying, and the cracked tune of the merry-go-round and the thunder of a tractor engine starting up. 'Wonderful fun.' Then the bark of the dogs echoed it: 'Wonderful fun.'

The gay colouring of the booths, the striped walls of the snake-pit tent, whirled together as the merry-go-round went round.

The children did not notice the first little wind till they saw the discarded paper bags and tickets dancing and then settling on the dusty trodden ground again. The big thunderhead clouds were coming up and it was very hot.

The people in the crowd felt the wind suddenly cooling the perspiration on their faces and down hot backs, but the children, swinging wide on the wooden horses, had already been cooled by the wind which the merry-go-round made. Fair children, dark children, mousy-brown children and one with hair of flaring red; children in bright pink frocks and children in coloured shorts and Wild West shirts, children in riding clothes; were swinging round through the air beside the gay show crowd, taking no notice of the wind that fluttered the awnings and lifted the coloured papers on the ground.

Joanna and Alex, holding Buckwong and The

Banjo and watching the pony ring, noticed it, and though Joanna's feeling about David had died down since the two events in which he had ridden, the gusts of wind, and the advancing thunderheads coming up before them, made her anxiety leap up within her again.

'I think the storm will hold off,' said Alex. 'Here come the children and it's almost time for the "Boy Riders Under Twelve".'

'Then the girls, and then lunch,' said Joanna. 'I could do with a cup of coffee.'

She patted Buckwong, who was looking prick-eared towards the wind, and smiled as he whinnied to David. She smiled again when she saw David pull a silk cloth from his pocket and rub it over his boots before he mounted.

The class was announced over the microphone, and they watched David ride out.

Sally thrust her hands into her pockets. She jumped as she felt the leather case containing the kingfisher feather. David should have been carrying it for his event. It was too late to get it to him. All she said was:

'He's got very good riders against him. Real show riders, I mean.'

Joanna nodded. Even the Gilliats knew more about show riding than the twins, she thought, though David might be as good after cattle. She tried to study them all dispassionately. It was quite clear that the boy whom David had seen soon after they arrived—the boy on the beautiful bay pony—would win, and another bigger boy from down the river would come second. But as she watched them trotting, cantering and dismounting,

she could really only see David on the big black galloway, his blond head held high, his shoulders straight,
his hands light on Buckwong's mouth.

Sally knew just how much he was trying to look
like the pictures in *Equitation*, but it was his mother
who knew how nervous he was of making a fool of
himself.

Then suddenly it happened, as Joanna had somehow known it must. There was a great rumble of
thunder and an ear-splitting backfire from a tractor.
Buckwong reared. Joanna saw her son, just as once she
had seen his grandfather, on a rearing black horse, but
young David looked so small. Then Buckwong landed
on all four feet, put his head down and started to bolt.
It all happened in a flash, and in that flash Joanna swung
on to her own horse to head him off—and saw Sally
ahead of her, already galloping The Banjo at an angle
to Buckwong's wild rush.

Buckwong seemed to check his speed as he got
nearer to Banjo, and David started to pull him up.
Sally saw his intent, white face, his lips moving as he
spoke soothingly to his pony. The Banjo was reefing,
plunging, and then *he* started to move, ahead of Buckwong, in great bounding strides, then they were
galloping neck and neck.

Joanna gave a whistle of mingled dismay and
surprise, but out of the nearby crowd a man's voice
rose clear and loud.

'I'll put a fiver on the little girl.'

Laughter crackled round the watchers.

'Hang on, kids, you're doing well,' a voice shouted.

'They'll stick on'; a man came up behind Joanna, and Arthur Wilton and Alex were cantering up.

Two or three others joined them and formed a group of horses between the bolting galloways, as they raced right round the ground and the judging rings.

'A dead heat! It's going to be a dead heat!' Another voice rose from the watchers on the rails.

'So long as they don't fall off it's all right,' thought Joanna.

'Two to one on the black,' someone else called. 'He's drawing ahead!'

'No! A dead heat!'

The children, still galloping neck and neck, heard some of the voices above the general noise of the crowd, and lost their feeling of desperate foolishness and of fear, and began to realize it might be funny, at least for those watching, and had better be funny for them too!

It was just then, as he looked round again at the crowd on the rails, that David saw a black face grinning above a green blouse and a tartan skirt. He had to ride his 'race' to a finish, but the picture stamped itself on his mind—the black face, the shapeless body leaning on the white rails of the ring, the tartan skirt billowing forward.

As they succeeded in pulling up beside their parents, David whispered to Sally:

'Black Mag's back there! Look!'

Sally looked back and was sure, and remained sure afterwards, that she saw the old aborigine turning away from the ring and melting into the crowd.

It was impossible for the twins simply to go looking for Black Mag, which is what they would have liked to have done. Firstly they had to laugh and talk to the people who, with their parents, had formed the group to stop the bolting ponies—try to behave as if they had felt neither desperately foolish nor afraid. Secondly David had to ride back to the collection of 'Boy Riders Under Twelve' and congratulate the winner.

Sally quickly leant forward and pressed the case with the kingfisher feather in it into his hand.

'You should have had this,' she said. 'It might never have happened. Anyway, it'll be a help now.'

David grinned, then he bent over and whispered to his mother:

'Black Mag's somewhere over there,' and rode back with his head high, and the kingfisher feather safely in his pocket. He congratulated the boy on the lovely bay.

Joanna and Sally rode round the ring, but could see no sign of the old lubra. Then Joanna walked with Alex through the crowds trying to find her. They did not like to ask anyone if they had seen her because somehow or other the story of her speaking to the children at the bridge had got around, and also the fact that no one except the Danes had seen her at all. Joanna had a weird feeling now that she would have been seen by no one but the twins—and certainly not a single person to whom they spoke said anything about an old lubra standing on the rails of the ring.

Then all of a sudden Joanna saw her in the milling crowd near the merry-go-round. One minute she was not there and the next minute she was, and though she was not very close, Joanna could hear her voice saying: 'Over the mountains, over the mountains,' and then she seemed to fade into the crowd, and was gone, completely gone, before Joanna could even point her out to Alex.

* * * * *

When the show was over, and the thunder crashing louder and louder, the Danes started to ride home, while old Jackie drove Dolly in the Land Rover. The twins' dreams of bringing home a blue ribbon or two had blown away in the storm, but the day had been very exciting, almost too much so, and David, for one, was sure that the kingfisher feather, even though he had failed to carry it at the time, was all that had turned his disaster into a joke.

When Joanna told of Black Mag's repeated phrase, 'Over the mountains, over the mountains', Alex listened with a puzzled expression and then said:

' Well, we may soon know what she means, because I have, just a few minutes ago, arranged with Norman Beatty, who is over from Adaminaby, to inspect a hundred two-year-old bullocks near Kiandra in a week's time.'

11 : 'Over the mountains'

A NOISE like wood screeving against wood sounded through the darkness before the dawn.

'Brolgas are on the move,' said Sally.

It came again, just the sound, not even a moving shadow in the dark. She imagined the great birds—knowing that their huge grey wings were slowly beating the cold air, that their long grey necks were outstretched, right to the red tops of their heads, and their beaks pointing forward; knowing that their legs and feet, with soles upturned, were stretched out behind—but she could see nothing. The birds went by, invisible.

'Brolgas flying through the dark,' she said thoughtfully. 'Listen to them!'

'They're quite close to the house,' said David. 'Just flying round the hill.'

They both lay on their faces, bedclothes pulled up to the backs of their heads, and peered out of the windows into the dark. The screeving noise came again, and further away a fox barked. Sally shivered. Dawn would come, but now they were surrounded by the mysterious and immense night.

'It'll be time to get up soon,' she whispered. 'I wonder what is going to happen "over the mountains" today? It certainly has been an exciting summer. It has seemed as if our meeting with old Black Mag, or whoever she was, has made everything seem even more alive than usual. . . .'

'And then seeing her again at the show,' said David, 'but I wonder why she didn't include my fight with Rickie in her prophecy of what was going to happen to us? It'll be Easter soon and Rickie'll be home again.'

'No, Black Mag never mentioned anything about that,' Sally laughed, 'but, after all, she did speak as if there could be many other things that she hadn't named.'

'Yes,' David answered, 'and I think that when she said she hadn't seen us at the Dragon-fly Cave it meant that she didn't know if we would get through all the dangers—and if we find the Dragon-fly Cave we are safely through.'

'Are you two awake?' Joanna's voice came from the doorway.

H

'Been awake for a minute or two. I think the brolgas woke us.' David sat up. 'Is it time to get dressed?'

Joanna walked across the room towards them, shining her torch.

'Dawn is just coming,' said Sally. 'There's a faint light over the mountains. Oh, Mummy, how exciting to be going up into the hills to inspect young cattle!'

Joanna laughed.

They had a very early breakfast, shivering as they watched the sun come over the Broadway Tom and glitter on the first shining mist of autumn. Then they packed billies and lunch into the back and squeezed into the front themselves, and away they went, headed for Walumba Creek and Woolsey Gap, for Toolong River, for the Fifteen Mile Spur and Lorna Doone on the Tumut River, and then Kiandra.

After three-quarters of an hour on the New South Wales river road, and on tracks through paddocks and over creeks that could be treacherous in wet seasons, they were going through a rough wooden gate at The Square and turning into the bush. The twins both leapt out to open the gate, wanting to be right there, in the start of it. Then the Land Rover was rattling over the stony road by tall stringy barks, by the kunzea bushes that, in spring, make drifts of fluffy mauve flowers up and down the ridges.

They stopped when they came to the Yellow Bog Creek, below the big climb. David and Sally ran up the little flat where Christmas bush flowers in summer, and crossed the creek on a big fallen tree.

David stood on the end of the log, holding on to a dead branch.

'Look at that little slab hut, Sal.'

Sally peeped over his shoulder at a derelict-looking hut, with its bark-shingle roof that no longer seemed weatherproof, and the tumble-down bench outside.

'I suppose it's a cattleman's hut,' she said, 'but it looks eerie. It's too low down for the real snow-leases. Perhaps a hermit lived here?'

'A lonely place to be on your own,' David muttered.

A coo-ee came from the Land Rover. David, feeling that he must look into the hut, leapt off the tree and ran across to it, Sally after him.

The door was fastened with a rusty bolt; it was difficult to open it. Neither could say why they wanted to peer in through the gloom at the rickety table inside and the collapsing bunk against the wall—and what they saw was an old, old vision of the loneliness of the Australian Bush.

They ran back to the Land Rover, racing over the fallen tree, smelling the lovely smell of the peppermints, the sharp tang of mint bush.

Their father smiled at them.

'Yes, that's a lonely-looking shack, on the Yellow Bog. Most of the huts have four or six bunks and great, wide fireplaces, and you can imagine half a dozen cattlemen yarning round the fire at night.' He turned to Joanna. 'You and I have listened to many a tale, while the mountain wind sighed in the trees outside, haven't we?'

Joanna smiled happily.

'We have indeed,' she said.

Just then the track started going up very steeply.

'Here we go,' Alex said.

Up they went and it seemed as if the Land Rover was rearing. Sally and David held on to the bar above the dashboard and watched as they climbed round a hairpin bend, then up and round another on a loose, stony surface.

'Phew!' David whistled. 'That was a climb!'

'It'll be a beautiful road by this time next year,' his father chuckled.

Then, out of the bush, as they drove along, stepped two horsemen with smart, silver-studded bridles and shining bits.

'Hullo! Where have they come from?' Sally looked at them curiously.

Alex pulled up the Rover and waited till the strange riders passed. The two men stopped several feet away, with their reins loose on their horses' necks.

'A dry autumn,' the smaller man said, and both of them looked penetratingly at the family in the Land Rover.

Alex Dane moved his brown hands on the steering wheel.

'Good travelling weather,' he said.

Joanna realized that he had given that answer on purpose, to seem as if they did not live quite close. She, too, had thought the men seemed strange. Then surprising words came from the bigger, younger man, whose skin was dark and shot through with rosy warmth, and who rode with the consummate ease with which some aborigines ride.

'There's nothing better than travelling over the mountains,' he said, 'but I expected you to be riding. There are some things you only see if you ride or go on foot.'

Then both riders shook the reins of their shiny bridles, and calling out: 'Well, so long,' over their shoulders, they rode on down the track.

'How right he is,' said Alex, 'but still . . .' and he let the clutch of the Land Rover in, and drove on slowly.

'Who on earth could they have been?' asked David.

Neither of his parents answered because they were both thinking over the words: 'I expected you to be riding. . . .'

They reached Woolsey Gap, the top of the main climb, and from there they could see across miles of rolling snowgrass mountains, and the twins stood gazing out over the lonely land—grey-green for snowgrass, grey-green for mystery. Each one stood for a moment imagining what it would be like to be riding over those hills, steadily riding over hill after hill towards the blue Monaro; imagining the swinging stride of their ponies, hooves soundless on the springy snowgrass; imagining the noonday smoke of their fire spiralling up beside a small and secret creek. They were still thinking that some day the mountains would be theirs, in just that way—or they the mountains'—as they raced down the clear hillside where a dozen tiny waterways and many spagnum soaks were the head of a creek that flowed down to the Toolong River. Over the water they leapt and danced. They pressed the squelching spagnum, they found pink and white everlastings and the bigger golden ones, they drank the freezing water.

Their road, after crossing the cold Toolong River, went up and down over the lonely, silent hills where somehow it seemed that no road should go. When at last they reached the Kiandra country they found that in spite of the gold rush that had been there many years ago, and in spite of the nearby works of the Snowy Mountains Scheme, the rolling hills were even more weird and lonely, as though the land could never really waken from the profound silence of its winter deep in snow.

Instead of running with wild exuberance as soon as they got out of the Land Rover, the twins simply stood and looked. They felt the weird ghostliness of the empty land, they listened to the silence that was broken only by the harsh cry of a crow.

The mob of young cattle were not far away, and Mr. Beatty came riding over, leading two horses, on which he suggested Joanna and Alex should ride to inspect them.

Joanna looked worried. She had not expected the courtesy of a horse for herself, and really did not wish to leave the twins.

'They will be all right,' said their father. 'They can get the fire laid down by the creek. I put firewood in the Land Rover.' He grinned at Mr. Beatty, because there are only snowgum woods in some places, and those mostly high on ridges in this Kiandra country.

'Keep the Land Rover in sight if you do any scrambling about,' he said to the twins. 'This is easy country in which to get lost.'

Still looking doubtful, Joanna mounted and rode off with the two men, and the twins rummaged for firewood, but their father's last words were eating into them. David shivered. He thought how utterly lost one could be in these hills, where only the wind moved and where each rolling dome against the sky was so like another.

They made themselves busy, setting the fire by the bubbling, singing creek, hardly speaking a word to each other, but looking up often at the eerie, deeply attractive land.

They collected a few pieces of dry, twisted alpine scrub, and filled the billies at the creek. When everything was done they stood up and looked around to see where they would go—and still be sure of not getting lost.

'If we walk up the last ridge that we passed in the Rover, we'll strike some timber and could bring back extra firewood,' David said. 'I don't think we've got enough.'

All the way up the ridge they kept looking back to make sure they could still see the Land Rover. The hill was steep, the grass was springy and a cool wind blew. Their fears began to be forgotten. Below they could see the mob of young cattle, Shorthorn and Herefords, lovely reds and roans, bright against the snowgrass. They climbed on upwards till they saw, some distance off, a dead tree, partly tumbled down, as though struck by lightning.

'There'll be more timber there than we can carry,' said David. 'Let's take what we need down now.'

All amongst the tumbled branches a little white bush was flowering, and as they walked up to it they saw a cloud of dragon-flies around it.

'What a mob!' David said, amazed.

Sally watched the gauze shimmer of their wings in the sunlight.

'Never seen as many outside the garden. . . . They must have meant something to the aborigines, or there wouldn't be a Dragon-fly Cave.' Then she added slowly: 'I wonder if we could be anywhere near it?'

David was wondering the same thing while he walked among the dragon-flies in a dream, as though trying to get a secret from them. And then, there at his feet, as he stood in the shimmering glitter of the wings, was a little track through the snowgrass.

'Look, Sally!' he said. 'Where could this lead?'

'The dragon-flies seem to be going along it,' Sally murmured. She looked down the slope: the road could be seen, but the Land Rover was hidden by a curve of ridge. Further away, the mob of cattle were plainly visible. 'I suppose we could safely follow it for a little way,' she said.

The track wandered across the main spur, across and upwards. The mob of cattle became hidden from view by trees, and the Land Rover did not come back into sight: the road was still there, far below. While they could see it, Sally knew they were really quite safe. Together they strode along the track, light-footed, gay.

'We'll pick up the firewood on the way back,' said David.

They had not been walking for much more than five minutes when their little path most surprisingly ran into what seemed a partly overgrown buggy-track.

'How queer!' Sally exclaimed.

'Extremely queer,' said David. 'Surely no one can ever come up here in a buggy or sulky now.'

Sally stood twisting the toe of one boot in the black earth, frowning. David had his eyes fixed on the ground and he was bending right over. He moved along a few paces, then a few more.

'I thought so! There are the wheel-marks of a sulky, and hoof-marks too! No one drives a sulky now except Black Mag!' Just then the sun went under a cloud. 'Hullo!' he said. 'Weather's not quite so perfect.'

Sally looked up, studying the sky.

'Only a small cloud, but there are more and more of them coming up from the north.'

David had gone a few more steps.

'The wheel-marks are plainer here,' he said. 'It's a shod horse.' He was so excited that he barely noticed the sun vanishing or reappearing again.

'It's not a very fresh track,' said Sally.

'No, but I don't think it's very old. Come on, let's go!'

'Better leave some mark on our own little path back to the dragon-fly tree, in case there are lots of paths.'

'Perhaps you're right.'

They drew arrows in the black earth and they dragged a twisted, dead snowgum limb and balanced it against a bitter pea bush at the start of the path. Then they set off along the wheel-marks.

'We must hurry,' Sally muttered, head down, watching the tracks. 'We shouldn't be too long away from the Land Rover. They'll only take about three-quarters of an hour or an hour looking at the cattle and talking.'

David glanced at his watch.

'It's only twenty minutes since we left, though it seems longer, but we'll have to hurry.'

They broke into a jogtrot along the 'road' as it climbed gradually up a spur towards the main ridge-top, but before they reached the top they were breathless and had to walk for a while. There were more trees along the top of the ridge, but the children could tell they did not go far down the other side. The sulky marks continued, sometimes seeming fresh, sometimes very old, sometimes clear, sometimes vanishing when the tussocks of snowgrass had encroached on the 'road'.

'The weather's getting worse,' said Sally, a feeling of foreboding making her footsteps slow.

'We'll only go a little further.' David started to jog again, and it was easier going, along the ridge-top.

Presently the 'road' turned off the ridge and down the other side, out of the trees into the bare and rolling hills, dropping quickly and vanishing from sight under the snout of a short spur. The wind, which carried up the grey clouds, blew chill against their hot bodies.

David looked at his watch again. Of course they were doing wrong, the sort of wrong that they had always been trained not to do.

'We'll just go down and round that corner, and if we don't see anything we will *have* to turn back then.'

Sally watched the ragged, wispy edges of the clouds and thought they could spread out into a mist the colour of the hills. The queer feeling of foreboding urged her both to go back and to run forward to see what was hidden from sight.

'Come on,' said David, and they both ran down the 'road'.

Almost immediately they saw the remains of an old aqueduct running across the hill, and two over-grown mines with the rotten remains of heavy planks lying across them.

'Wonder if there's any gold left?' David called out, but neither of them slackened speed. Down and round the spur snout they ran, and there they stopped dead.

There were two old shacks with tumbled-in roofs, open doors and windows like unseeing eyes. Blank and empty, the huts stood, and only the wind moved through them.

'There's one that isn't a ruin, lower down.' Sally pointed to it.

It was just then that they saw an old man stooped over a little trickling creek, and holding a washing cradle in his hands.

'So you hev come,' he said, straightening up and staring at them. 'So you hev come out of the bright day that is clouding. But there should have been a third.'

'Have you seen an old aborigine woman go by in a sulky?' Sally asked politely.

'Oh aye, she came . . . fifty years ago or sixty . . . when I war no more'n a boy, but it seems like on'y yesterday. . . . Mebbe it was. She said you'd be coming.'

'Do you know where the Dragon-fly Cave is?' asked David, wondering whether the weird old man was aboriginal or Chinese, or just old, so old that he was part of the hills.

'You'll find the Dragon-fly Cave, or you may do, if you get through the flood. Listen to the roar o' the flood. Listen to the cry of the birds, they'll tell you the way, an' watch the kangaroos, they go past it.' He raised his hand. 'Listen!' he said. 'Listen!'

The birds came crying, crying through the grey sky. Three black cockatoos came, black against the clouds. They flew overhead with their tails barred with yellow, and back along the path.

'Follow 'em. They cry o' clouds that'll come. Follow 'em, so black like the storm,' the old man said.

Sally, in sudden fear, as the clouds drifted round, took David's arm.

'We'll never see the track if we don't go quickly,' she said.

'Is the Dragon-fly Cave near here?' David asked.

'No! Miles 'n' miles away,' the old man answered. 'Go now! Go!'

They turned and ran up the 'road'.

12 : Cry the black cockatoos!

SALLY looked up the spur. Already the top of it was twisting to a different shape, fading, blending into the grey-green cloud. She dropped her eyes hastily to the 'road'. It was there, at her feet still—two half-overgrown wheel-tracks, and the track for the horses' hooves. She felt that it was not quite an ordinary road, and that it, too, might climb into the clouds and blow away in the wind, or be twisted round so that it led them right away from the friendly seeming Land Rover and the mob of cattle. She held on to the kingfisher feather in its leather case, deep in her jodhpur pocket. Far ahead she heard the weird crying of the black cockatoos, and they filled her with fear. Once she bent down and touched the snowgrass and the ground with her hand, to be certain that it was solidly there, the firm, grey-green mountain.

She and David raced up the hill panting and getting very tired. When she looked back the clouds had all gathered together. It was not just imagination, there *was* a greeny heart to the big cloud.

'A greeny cloud means hail,' she said to herself, and her feet and her pounding heart beat out the words: 'means hail, means hail, means hail', till it seemed that the black cockatoos, away ahead in the mist, screamed 'hail! hail!'

The cloud swirled around them, and she touched the ground again, just to be sure.

'Do you think we'll get back again before the storm comes?' Sally panted.

'Dunno,' David answered. 'We didn't really come so far . . . we should make it,' but they both knew they had come further than they ought to have come, especially when there were clouds blowing up.

It did not take them long to reach the main ridge-top and the trees, but now the snowgums were starting to lash their boughs in a sudden wildness of the wind. Not one tree looked the same as it had looked when they came down. Now the twisted limbs beat, and thrashed, and strained away from the gnarled trunks. The dark green leaves were sometimes black, some-times glittering.

'Soon we ought to be able to see the road below

if the clouds haven't flowed into the valley,' David said.

'Or if this cloud behind us doesn't catch us up completely,' added Sally. 'It could make everything too misty for us even to see *this* "road".'

'I know,' David answered.

Among the trees they could still see the old 'road', but when it left the top of the ridge to go down the side up which they had climbed from the Land Rover, they left the shelter and suddenly found themselves in thick, swirling grey cloud, with the grey ground dropping away invisibly, and no connected signs of the track. Behind them the wind wailed in the snow-gums. The last terrifying cry of the black cockatoos came from far ahead.

The twins stopped, dismayed.

David pulled himself together and tried to look confident. 'I'll go on a yard or two, and see if the wheel-tracks are easier to pick up farther on. You stay here.'

From two or three yards ahead he called:

'Come on. I think this is still all right.'

When he went on again Sally looked at the shape-less, constantly changing land that blended with the swirling cloud, and the loneliness of those age-old Kiandra hills and plains gripped her. She wondered if they would ever find their way back. Fiercely she pushed down the panic that kept rising inside her.

They crept on, yard by yard, taking it in turns to go searching for the 'road', till at last they could find nothing that even resembled a track in snowgrass, and Sally said flatly:

'It's gone, and I can't help feeling that it really wasn't there. We should have found our arrows and our snowgum limb on the bush by this time, and there's nothing. . . .'

There was nothing, only the rolling, moving, grey-green hills and the moving clouds. They looked and looked, and could not tell hill from cloud, nor cloud from hill, and they were afraid.

They did not know that they had been twisted round by the cloud and the wind and had gone in the wrong direction altogether. They had heard their mother say 'No man's a bushman in a mist', but they had never fully imagined the cold, wet touch of the clouds, the sudden tearing, roaring wind, the blind feeling of walking in darkness, and ground suddenly dropping away so that sometimes there was nothing on which to tread, and the whole world was insubstantial. Nor had they known how desperately alone they could be in the dark cloud and the wind, and the wild, empty hills.

'It feels more than ever as though there is nothing in front of us,' said David after he had tried a few yards in another direction. 'I'm sure there is a big drop ahead. We had better stand still and hope the wind may blow the clouds apart in a moment, and let us see. The bad weather did come up quickly, it could blow away just the same.'

So they stood in the bleak cloud, and the wind, and the grey nothingness that yet touched them with wet, cold fingers, and they waited.

*   *   *   *   *

Joanna had been worried all the time. Even the lovely young cattle could not completely claim her attention. Firstly she had soon felt the change coming in the weather, and secondly she was afraid that the twins, expecting queer happenings, might forget all their training, and follow some will o' the wisp of a clue to the mystery of Black Mag—which was, of course, what had happened. Though Alex, who had a profound insight, had realized that something strange was contained in their meetings with the old woman whom they had laughingly called Black Mag, it was she who had been present when the aborigine spoke, and she knew that she felt more worried about all the mysterious trials and dangers than he did, felt more drawn into it all herself, and understood how deeply involved the twins felt.

The first clouds blew over the hill-top and she looked up at them anxiously, but Alex took no notice. She rode up beside him as she saw the clouds getting thicker and said she thought she should go back.

'No, we'll be through soon,' he said. 'The twins will be all right. They'll be at the Land Rover.'

After a while a half-aboriginal stockman who worked for Mr. Beatty rode alongside.

'Clouds gettin' thick,' he said. 'I seen your kids makin' up the hill. Maybe I better ride 'n' find 'em.'

'Yes,' said Joanna swiftly. 'I'll come too.'

She rode across to Alex and they exchanged whispers about the value of the bullocks and the price they should pay, then she rode off with the stockman up the silent Kiandra hills, and the stockman said never a

I

word except when he pointed to the greeny colour of
the cloud and said:

'Hail, then sun agen, but first hail.'

He seemed to know exactly the way the twins had
gone, and led on unerringly, up and across the ridge.
He pointed out the children's arrows just when the
cockatoos were flying over. Then the clouds poured
down on to the land, enfolding everything.

'They will be afraid,' said Joanna sharply.

'We'll find 'em,' came the answer, and the stockman
led on and on. After some time he called a wild, clear
'Coo-ee, coo-ee' that could not be muffled by any
cloud.

An answer came faintly back through the mist.

Joanna's hands were shaking. She gulped in a breath
of cold wind and cloud, and followed her guide. Several
times he gave a 'Coo-ee'. Each time the answer was
closer.

'Must be quick. Hail's comin',' the stockman said,
'an' follow carefully, we're goin' round a deep quarry
that gold came out of once.'

The quarry was invisible. Joanna could feel the
drop into nothingness, and then she saw the edge. The
children were standing right at the head of it.

'You found 'im?' asked the stockman, as he rode
up to them, and Joanna was so surprised that she did
not speak, only took hold of both their upstretched
hands.

'We found a man, old like the mountains,' answered
David.

'That's 'im. Jump up behind. Hail's comin'!' He

drew his horse up beside a log and Joanna did the same. Neither of the horses seemed to object to the extra weight, as David got behind the stockman and Sally behind her mother, but they did object to the hail that suddenly burst out of the greeny cloud in marbles of ice that beat relentlessly.

Joanna had such hard work to stop her horse bolting madly down the hillside in front of the flailing ice that she had no time to ask Sally anything—or to say anything about them going so far from the Land Rover.

All the way down she fought and struggled with the plunging horse, and she was breathless, as well as wet and cold and bruised from the hailstones, when they reached the road at the bottom. As they got to the Land Rover, before she could speak, Sally said:

'I'm dreadfully sorry, Mummy, that we went so far. It was just that we followed the sulky tracks because we were sure Black Mag had gone that way.'

Joanna had known that there was a compelling power in the words of the old lubra, a power that could make the twins go tearing off on a wild chase over the mountains, or brave queer dangers to find a cave and a feather. 'Yet,' she thought, 'even if it was Black Mag who led them off there was this half-aboriginal stockman who seemed to know all about where they had gone.' She knew she must tell them how wrong they had been, but her voice, when she spoke, said:

'Who was the old man?'

'He seemed as if he was just a part of the hills,' Sally answered. 'He was washing for gold, and I'm sure he expected you too.'

Then the stockman spoke again.

'The cattle've broken. We best stay on our horses and help.'

Joanna could not see anything, but the stockman seemed to be able to see through cloud and beyond human vision, or perhaps he simply knew what must happen that day. They rode on, with the children still holding on behind.

'Sun'll come again,' the stockman said, as the hail lightened.

'Had Black Mag been there?' Joanna asked Sally, over her shoulder.

'Sometime or other she had, because the old man said she had told him we would come.' Sally sounded puzzled. 'But he didn't know whether it was fifty or sixty years ago or just the other day. . . . He did say he expected three of us. . . .'

The stockman started to canter. For the first time Sally felt the wonderful springy snowgrass under the horse's cantering feet. She sat behind her mother, moving to the swing of the horse as it went swiftly over the partly invisible ground. The hail stopped and she was starting to get warm, starting to enjoy herself, even though the minutes, just past, when she and David stood alone in the dense cloud, would haunt her dreams for many a year.

As they got down the valley and heard the cattle, the stockman slowed up. Then out of the clouds appeared the tail of the mob, red beasts and roan, lowing their dislike of hail to the echoing, cloud-hidden hills.

The mob had gone in all directions, and the men had got them under control as soon as the hail stopped driving them, but it had been an exciting few minutes and Alex had not had time to worry much about the twins, or to think that they could be lost or hurt.

The twins soon realized this, and as they realized that, at least for the time, no hard words were likely to be said about their going off alone in this indeterminate country, especially when clouds were coming up, their nervous, guilty feeling faded. Each one felt, instead, the immense draw of that 'road' across the lonely hills, the deep compulsion that existed somewhere within Black Mag's prophecy.

13 : A feather from the blue bird
in flight

'I WISH we didn't have to do school today,' David said
wistfully.

'Oh well. Easter holidays start tomorrow,' his
mother smiled.

'And I am to give you another boxing lesson today,'
his father came in, grinning broadly. 'You'd better
hurry up and do your school work and have the lesson
because, for some unknown reason, Rickie and Margie
got off early and arrived home last night.'

'*Did* they?' asked Joanna.

'Yes, they did. I have been speaking to Brian on the phone, so I know.'

The great fight between the two boys had been made into a family joke, but both Joanna and Alex knew that, though David could laugh about it now, to him it was not really a joke. Being given such a beating by Rickie, who had been his friend, was a very bitter experience which had faded into the background only since the twins were lost in the storm. They knew also that Rickie's enmity now seemed to David as if it was in some way linked up with the trials of strength and courage foretold by Black Mag, and could only hope that in the holidays there would be the start of a better friendship again. The boxing lessons had been given in a spirit of fun.

The twins plodded away at the school work, finding it impossible to pay attention to problems related to a railway timetable or the area of an army camp.

It was more interesting to choose their own poem to add to their poetry books and illustrate. During this term they had to begin to find their way among the Australian poets, and now they took David Campbell's books and Judith Wright's from the shelves and searched for poems that would say something of the bush in summer, for summer had gone and it was regretted.

'Funnily enough,' said David, 'there are more poems that give the feeling of winter.'

'David Campbell comes from the Monaro, on the other side of the mountains,' Joanna told him, 'and Judith Wright from New England. Winter in both parts of the land would be hard with frost and snow, harder on the country than here, where we have the heavy river mists so often, but perhaps pleasanter to live through than are a couple of months of our winter.'

'I will choose "The End of Exploring",' said Sally. 'It has winter and it has summer, and it has something else too, as though he'd gone searching for something. . . .'

'Read some of it,' Joanna suggested.

Sally drew the book towards her and started to read clearly but rather without expression.

> 'But why go? The time waits deep for summer
> With the grain, for the ringed shade and sheep
> Cropping the silence while the swagmen sleep,
> Though on the height the ice-etched symbols
>   glimmer.'

She paused and looked up.

Joanna nodded.

'It is from here, more than over there, that one sees "the ice-etched symbols glimmer",' she said. 'Though I have seen the Range, from Rennix Gap, glittering with film crust. Read on, Sally!'

Sally took in a breath and went on:

> 'And the road? Go then; and smothered in the
>   snow,
> Or on the violet ridge where the ice-trees burn,
> Trust to your lucky heart you may return
> With love to dog-bark, gate, and sweet cock-crow.

'It's the last verse that sounds as if Black Mag had

been telling him to look for the Dragon-fly Cave,' Sally said and grinned.

'It does rather,' David laughed. 'There are lots of his poems I enjoy. Here's one called "Snowgums", Mummy; you read it to us.'

Again it was the last verse that held them in thrall:

'The powdered bloom along the bough
Wavers like a candle's breath;
Where snow falls softly into snow
Iris and rivers have their birth.'

Joanna put the book down. 'Well, you must write out the poems you choose now,' she said, and added in a rather wistful voice: 'There are so many wonderful ones to learn.'

While the twins settled down to write Joanna went to the kitchen to start weighing out the ingredients for shortbread. Dolly was just cutting tomatoes for a tomato pie, and she looked up as Joanna came in, smiling a greeting, but as she saw Joanna she could also see out of the window. Her face altered expression, and she said:

'Whist, Miss Joanna. Here comes young Rickie. Now, is he up to good or bad?'

'Oh, *blow!*' said Joanna. 'I'll not be able to cook now. I expect I'd better be with them.'

'Never you mind. We'll get cakes and biscuits done for Easter, all right. You run along, and keep them from scrapping.' Dolly's dear old face looked as it had looked when Joanna was a little girl herself. 'I reck'n if Rickie gets over the next two terms at school without bashing David badly they'll be great friends again.'

Joanna smiled at her and went out of the wire door.

'Hullo there, Rickie!' she called. 'Welcome home!'

'Hullo, Aunt Joanna!' the boy said. 'I've ridden over to see the twins.'

'They're still finishing their school work,' Joanna smiled. 'You seem to be home a day early.'

'Yes, we were lucky. Will they be long?' Rickie did not look very comfortable.

'They can finish this evening. Come and find them, they're on the front verandah.'

They walked along the path together and as they were rounding the corner Joanna called out:

'Twins! Here's Rickie. He's ridden over.' Just like a warning jay, she told herself, but she could not arrive on the steps with Rickie without letting them know.

The twins were still sitting at their places, one at the head and one at the side of the table, stiff and straight, with startled expressions on their faces, when she and Rickie reached the steps. There was a second's awkward silence before they said 'Hullo!' without any great enthusiasm, and pushed back their chairs.

'I expect Rickie would like a cool drink,' said Joanna. 'Sally, you could get lemonade and glasses, dear'; then she turned to Rickie. 'How's school been going?'

'Oh, all right,' he said. 'It's a pity that swimming and cricket are over.'

'How hard do they make you work?' Joanna asked with professional interest.

'Oh, I dunno,' Rickie said. 'Some masters whop it on to us.'

Joanna opened the twins' arithmetic textbook.

'Are you much beyond this?'

'Couldn't do those if I tried all day,' Rickie said; then his eyes fell on David's exercise book and the open poetry book. 'What on earth are you writing here, David?'

'Just a poem.' David's voice was stiff.

'Gosh!' said Rickie, his eyes running down a few lines. 'Do you *like* that stuff?'

Joanna, seeing the sudden fierce expression on his face as he came up against what he most likely thought was the 'queerness' of the Danes, and which yet made him jealous, quickly picked up an English grammar book for him to see.

'Can you stay to lunch, Rickie?' she asked, when he was safely looking at it. Just then the phone rang and she had to go to answer it. Jane's voice greeted her.

'Your line's been out of order. I've been trying to get on to you ever since Rickie left. Has he arrived?'

Joanna laughed.

'Yes, he has.'

'Oh dear, I meant to warn you! I hope they're not fighting. Rickie wanted to go over to make it up, but I have been afraid he might be feeling different by the time he got there, or that David couldn't just get around to making it up. . . .'

Joanna laughed again, even more weakly than the first time.

'I don't know whether he's still feeling the same—and I think David is a little cold. They're not fighting, and if he may stay to lunch I'll take them out for a ride.'

'That would be very nice,' Jane said, 'so long as he's not a nuisance. I would love to see him back pretty soon, though, because it's a long time since he was home, and I've made a special cake for him.'

'Righto,' said Joanna. 'Leave it to me, Jane dear, and I hope there will be no bloodshed!'

Sally had brought the drinks when she got back to the verandah, and the three children were eyeing one another more than coldly.

'That was your mother, Rickie,' said Joanna. 'She doesn't mind if you stay to lunch, but I know she'd like you home right afterwards. What about us all going for a ride down to the river before lunch, if the twins catch their ponies?'

'Good idea,' said David. 'It's warm enough to swim, isn't it?'

Rickie whistled.

Joanna looked at him with a grin.

'Each day has seemed as if it was going to be the last. The water really is freezing.'

'I should think it would be,' Rickie said.

Joanna saw the first sign of enjoyment in David's face, and realized that Rickie would be forced to freeze if possible.

'I'll get some togs for you,' David said.

*　　*　　*　　*　　*

It did not take long to catch The Banjo and Buckwong and Joanna's pony, and they were soon, all four, riding down the horse paddock.

'Let's go to one of the deep bends,' David said, and he looked down on to the river flats, adding with surprise: 'Must have been a frost on the flats. The smart weed's turning.'

'It'll be cold, cold, cold,' chanted Sally.

The loops of the river glistened, the golden leaves shone, and the very air seemed to shine above the shining land. High in the sky a huge flock of birds gleamed as they wheeled, and David gave a shout.

'Look! They're pelicans!'

Rickie screwed up his eyes.

'Seem to be about a hundred.'

'There are thirty-six,' said David.

Rickie looked round at him suspiciously.

'Go on,' he said.

'There are,' David grinned, and then, to stop any argument, Joanna announced that she made them thirty-six too.

'Count them in twos, like cattle, Rickie,' she smiled.

'Why on earth do you get so much fun out of the birds?' Rickie asked suddenly.

The twins looked a little taken aback.

'I don't know,' Sally answered. 'We do, though! Perhaps it is because they're so beautiful.'

'They are free—in the air . . .' David's forehead was puckered.

'I think those are two of the reasons,' Joanna joined in. 'I've wondered myself, what it is about birds, and I've thought that it may be that they are so perfect—in flight, in song, in colouring—or, for instance, a kingfisher diving. . . .'

'It is so fascinating to think of rainbow birds and dollar birds going as far north as Malaya during our winter, too,' said Sally, 'and the terrific journey of the swifts . . . and why do diamond sparrows only come sometimes? . . .'

'And think of brolgas dancing by moonlight,' David murmured. His voice was very low, but Joanna heard, and knew that he had forgotten Rickie for the moment and was trying to imagine what 'the Brolga Moon' could be.

'There are often three brolgas on the reserve by our gate,' said Rickie.

'Are they still there?' asked Joanna. 'They used to be there, years ago, solemnly moving on the edge of our mob of cattle, or flying slowly away.'

The horses splashed through the runner, and the water shone as it flew up. It was indeed a shining world, yet one that would soon be sombre with winter.

They cut across the first river point, and then turned into the next, riding along its topmost bank, passing under willows and great, spreading redgums. When they were right at the point they went to find shade in which to tie their ponies.

Rickie went towards the willows at the river's bank, and had tied his little chestnut on to an old fence post when he looked up through the branches and the golden leaves and saw a kingfisher out above the bright water, cleaning its feathers. He beckoned David, who was walking towards him, and pointed to the kingfisher. Both David and Sally came quietly and swiftly.

They stood silently watching. The bird stopped

cleaning itself and moved its head and body straight up and down, over and over again, as though it had springs at the top of its legs. The twins knew that kingfishers behaved like that if they saw anything strange, so they stood absolutely still. Then it started to clean itself again, parting all the feathers with its long beak, the chestnut-red breast feathers and the dark blue wing feathers, even round on the dark blue back. One wing seemed to give him immense trouble.

As they watched, the children knew Joanna had come up too, but she made no sound, and this time the kingfisher did not spring up and down nervously, but just kept cleaning its left wing. Then suddenly it was as though something called him from the other side of the water. He flew across the river, and in a flash he was no longer dark blue and chestnut, but rosy red and a living glory of blue, bright and soft, yet deep.

' "Mary's colour",' thought Joanna.

At that moment a blue feather fell, floating down from the left wing, and landed on the shining surface of the stream.

The three Danes jumped as if they'd been bitten. Then David and Sally started flinging off their boots.

'I'll watch it while you get into your togs,' Joanna said.

Even as she spoke, the feather, which had been moving slowly downstream, got caught up in a current that swung it towards the deep pool in the curve of the opposite bank.

'Oh, quick!' gasped David.

By the time he and Sally had run and let themselves in upstream, they could no longer see the feather.

'It'll be hard to see from the water,' said Joanna, by way of explanation to Rickie, who stood looking amazed. 'I'll get my horse.'

She ran back to her pony, hooked off her boots on a log, and leapt into the saddle, cantering back to the water's edge, and straight in towards the deep curve and the two blond heads. A great splash rose up around her, then she forced the pony to go quickly across the shallow part of the river.

'There it is,' she called, pointing, and standing in her stirrups. 'Keep your eyes open for any snags.'

Neither of the twins heard. Joanna pushed her pony in further. She could see the feather quite plainly now, caught for a moment in a circling eddy in the centre of the deep pool. The water looked dark, where it was deep, and it was hard to tell if there were any snags. As David raised his head for a breath, she called:

'Keep your eyes open and watch for snags.'

David heard her and realized for the first time that she was there. He lifted his head again.

'Can you see the feather?' he called, and Sally, hearing his voice, stopped swimming too.

'In the centre of the pool, going round and round,' Joanna answered.

Rickie had put on his bathing-trunks and was standing on the bank, watching.

'There it is,' cried Sally, and shot forward. In a moment she was waving the feather gaily.

'I'm nearly frozen,' said David, and Rickie could hear the laughter in his voice, and the excitement.

'You carry it, Mummy,' Sally called.

The twins swam towards her, till they could put their feet on the bottom, Sally carrying the feather out of the water. They walked a few steps to their mother, bracing themselves against the current. Joanna stooped from the saddle and took the deep blue wing-feather in her hand. Then, when the children were clear of her pony, she turned and rode back, her socks and trouser-legs wet but her face bright with excitement.

She saw the puzzled expression on Rickie's face, as she rode to the bank, and she swung off and flung an arm round his shoulders.

'We're mad, aren't we, Rickie! But it is quite important in the Dane family, at present, to have a king-fisher feather—a token of good luck. And it was you who saw the kingfisher first. . . .'

'So you've done us a good turn,' said David, breathless from effort and from the cold. He walked out of the water, and he had forgotten the fight with Rickie, forgotten that he had meant to challenge him to a long race in the freezing river, and could only feel gloriously excited. They had another feather from 'the blue bird in flight', an azure kingfisher had almost deliberately dropped it for them.

Joanna got into her bathing-suit and then ran into the icy water with the three children, and as the spray spangled up all around them, she found herself thinking how, over the months, the old lubra's words were slowly coming true.

K

14 : Untold secrets in the wind and the snow

THE COLD seemed almost to be biting into their faces and hands as the twins and their mother rode along the banks of the steely grey river. When the bitter wind from the south blew, the golden leaves of the basket willows floated down on to the water and were carried away, and the dry reeds rustled. The sweet brown reed warblers had gone.

'Winter has come,' Joanna said, thrusting her cold right hand into her trouser pocket. 'And it's too early for it to be as cold as this.' The wind lifted the hood of her old ski jacket. 'Brr!' she said.

'Never mind, Mummy,' David laughed. 'Winter means snow, and we'll get some ski-ing.'

'Yes,' she said and her face lit up, 'perhaps quite a lot this year.'

They rode through a number of cows that had been put in the paddock for the winter after their calves were weaned. They looked at them all critically, and counted as they rode.

'Seventy-nine, I get,' said Sally.

'I think that's right.' Joanna turned to David. 'What do you get?'

'The same,' he replied. 'Some of them look a bit poor.'

'M'm. The younger ones that have just reared their first calf. I hope, for their sake, that the winter's not going to be too hard. That's ninety-four in all, with the ones near the lagoon.'

In a wattle tree that leant over the river a round, grey thrush whistled its wonderful song.

'He is a joy in winter,' said Joanna suddenly, as if she were counting her blessings, but after all it was true that this winter would not be so bad. The cold, and the mist, and the rain were not unbearable when one could take an active part in the work with the stock and the land, and now the twins were older it was possible to get out much more. And now they were old enough to take ski-ing often—and there was the road to the mountains.

A finger of cold sunlight lay along the furthest river point.

'Let's hurry,' said Sally, 'so that we get there before even that patch of sun goes, but we'll have to take it easy when we're nearly there because the plovers may be dancing—it's about the right time of year.'

They rode on, cantering for a while, and then slowing down as they counted nineteen more cows, then cantering again till they were near the banks of the lagoon where, even in Joanna's memory, the river had run, and which was now a favourite haunt of ducks and swans. Here the sunlight was brittle-bright, but cheering. The swans and ducks and a few ibis flew up—their bodies bright against the sombre sky.

'Listen!' David held up a hand. 'I do hear a great many plovers.'

'They were round the other side last year,' Sally said.

There, on the open, grassy flat, on the other side of the lagoon, they saw over thirty plovers, all congregated together, then suddenly rising, all the brown and white birds flying, crying. Their mournful cries filled the air, and yet did not seem to have quite the same sadness as one single cry does, when it sounds through the darkness of the night.

They wheeled and wheeled again, then landed on the grass, close together, before taking off once more to fly and cry in a pattern of brown and white and black-tipped wings. Over and over again they landed and took off and flew above the riders, filling the air with their constant, haunting cries.

David looked up restlessly, feeling that if he listened hard enough he would understand what they meant.

His mother was the first to speak.

'It is like a ceremonial corroboree,' she said. 'We have never seen so many before.'

'I wonder,' said Sally slowly, 'if we are really *seeing* things more this year, or whether everything is being especially wonderful?'

Joanna knew exactly what she meant and what the twins were thinking, but did not like to show that she thought the same; that she, too, felt that Black Mag had in some way cast over their world a light that had never shone before.

The one shaft of sunlight was soon blocked by the massing clouds, and the Danes moved on, counting the cows, looking carefully at them all. As they rode, the clouds were gathering and becoming darker and darker, till, in the south, there was an immense black cloud whose centre seemed pulled backwards, into the heart of the hills.

'We must not be too long,' said Joanna. 'The count is right, and we'd better get home. There's going to be a big storm from the south. Snow on the hills, I should think.'

'That cloud looks as if it could suck us up into itself,' Sally said.

'And drop us out the other side on to Pinnabar or the Pilot,' laughed David, and they all saw in their minds a picture of the sharp-pointed mountain, the Pilot and the splendid dome of Mount Pinnabar.

'We'll see that country under snow this year,' Joanna said, and quoted the poem they had loved so much: ' "Where iris and rivers have their birth".'

'Well, at any rate, where the Murray River is born,' David said.

'The birds are getting restless: they know there's a storm coming,' said Sally.

They watched the magpies beating against the wind, screaming, and then letting themselves be swept before it. Magpie larks were flying into the thick bands of willows. Wagtails and robins were in the trees along the runner, no longer hawking the air. Kurrawongs, the great mountain magpies, called and called in the wild wind.

'Listen to the cry of the birds,' the old man of the mountains had said, and Sally and David had listened and listened, watched and watched, and it seemed as if they were always on the brink of understanding something, but they could not have told what. Now, as they rode home, being almost blown up the hill into the horse paddock, the birds told them unmistakably of the storm that would come. Far away on the flats they could hear some brolgas calling, and then six or seven gang-gangs flew round the hill, headed towards the forested paddocks, tossed on the wind, screeching.

'Gang-gangs! Storm is coming,' Sally called gaily.

'Storm already raging in the mountains,' said Joanna, and she felt like a taut wire moving to the force of the wind, taut and waiting. . . .

With frozen fingers David undid the stable gate, frozen fingers fumbled at the buckles on girths and bridles. They brushed down the ponies quickly, talking to them, petting them, grooming away imaginary sweat.

'Let's look at the cloud from the top of the hill,

Mummy,' Sally said, her eyes bright, her hair wild, and they ran, hand in hand, up from the stable yard, over the drive, and on to the crest of the hill where the full force of the wind caught them.

There, on the other side of the hill, blowing, came a stream of golden leaves as though from the deep, dark centre of the black cloud, golden out of the black, leaves flying with such force that it seemed they were shot from the cloud. Below was the great golden elm.

'The elm tree is being stripped,' David shouted against the wind.

'But look how lovely the leaves are!' cried Sally, and she raced towards them. Then suddenly she turned and catherine-wheeled back—legs in fawn jodhpurs, arms in blue jersey, spinning, a wheel spun in the wind among the hurtling leaves.

Joanna stopped quite still, pressed against the icy gale. It seemed as if there was some immense significance in the afternoon. She felt sure that the storm meant a great deal to them, but it was not only that. First there had been the corroboree of the plovers, then the crying, wind-flying birds, now the golden leaves from the black centre of the cloud and Sally spinning amongst them. She watched and waited, pressed against the power of the gale, and did not know why she was waiting. Did she wait for a voice in the wind, or was it just to see Sally wind-spun with the leaves?

Sally landed on her feet beside her, laughing, and the spell which had held Joanna lost its intensity. She sighed.

'I'll go and make some tea. A warm drink. . . .

Will you both come in in a minute?' She turned and walked along to the house.

She was only just out of sight and out of hearing when the twins realized that someone was riding up the drive. They could hear neither hoof-fall nor jangle of bit in the noise of the wind, but suddenly they both looked towards the gate as though some sound had come to them. There, they were sure, was the bigger of the two flashy-looking men who had appeared out of the bush on the Yellow Bog spur. Even when he was only half-way along the drive they could see how shiny his bridle and saddle were. They stood as though frozen, and the man rode right up to them before he spoke.

'D'you know if three red bulls branded with the old Munyang brand hev been seen hereabouts?' he asked.

David felt as if he was frozen into silence, but he managed to force out his voice.

'No strange red bulls have been here since last January,' he answered, 'unless my father has seen any today,' and he was just going to add, 'but he's not in yet,' when he thought he'd better keep quiet.

'Ah well, I'd best keep going,' the man said, smiling, then asked: 'D'you know anything? There's going to be a storm, I would guess.'

'The gang-gangs and kurrawongs seem to think there's snow coming in the mountains,' David said.

'Ah ha! You've been listening to the birds, the way you were told,' the man laughed.

David and Sally both stiffened and looked suspiciously at the man with his dark skin and the rosy glow that shone through it, but he just went on speaking.

'A cloud blacker than the lubra of the night means snow too,' he said. 'Know the birds, know the animals, know the trees and the whispering dry grass: know the clouds and the winds: understand snow: every one of them will tell you.'

'Tell what?' Sally asked quite sharply.

'All the untold secrets that the snow hides, they are more precious than the gold that the white men dug out of our hills,' the strange man answered. 'I must go to look for my bulls. When the plovers hold corroboree it is not long till the Brolga Moon. When snow falls there must some time be flood.'

Then some words suddenly burst from David.

'Please tell us where to find the Dragon-fly Cave.'

'The Dragon-fly Cave is only found when the untold secrets are whispered in the wind and the snow, roared in the floods. . . .' And the man was going almost as if he was borne on a veering whirl of wind.

Sally and David ran beside his stirrups.

'How shall we look for it?' David called against the wind, and Sally's voice was nearly carried away as she cried:

'Where is Black Mag?'

The man only laughed, and with a jangle of his silver-studded bridle shot away from them at a canter.

That night the rain came and the snow fell on the mountains. David went out and stood beside the warm, bright-lit house in the immensity of the winter storm that whirled up and down the valleys and howled round the foothills and over the Alps.

15 : Skier like a hawk descending

WHEN THE RAIN stopped, and the clouds cleared away, the mountains were deeply covered in snow, aloof and white above the green land. There were three fine days with windy skies, and then clouds, shaped like great fish, swam above the mountains in the evening, and by next day it was raining again. Two days later, while listening to the news from the Snowy Mountain Authority on the wireless, Alex Dane heard that another five inches of snow had fallen. It was also announced that the road over Dead Horse Gap was open only to four-wheel-drive vehicles.

He switched off the wireless and turned round, his eyes bright and dancing.

'We'll go ski-ing,' he said. 'It's not often that we ski in May.'

The weather was fining up by midday, and the glass rising fast. They had collected their skis, sticks and boots, and searched for all their clothes that had been put away in moth-proof bags. By night-time the glass was still rising, and the stars were hard and bright.

'I think it will be all right,' said Joanna as she walked back into the house after studying the night. 'Let's leave before dawn.'

'Good idea,' said Alex. 'If the weather doesn't hold, clouds may blow up at midday, but we'll have had lots of ski-ing by then.'

So it was dark still when they left, except for the last of the moonlight, and it seemed that the cold was intense, though Joanna knew that this was nothing to the cold that would come in June and July and August.

Sally touched the horse-trough and found a thin surface of ice.

'Yes, it is freezing,' her father said, 'but not really hard. We have left for ski-ing before the dawn when our footsteps rang on the ground as though it were iron, and, with the light, it looked as if snow had fallen all over the land.'

'Frost?' asked David.

'Yes, frost.'

Joanna laughed.

'You wait till mid-winter. Perhaps we may make a dawn start some time then,' she said, and she whistled

happily to herself as they carefully balanced the two
thermos flasks in the back of the Land Rover, one in
the spare tyre and one inside a rubber boot, and piled
into the front seat themselves.

Then they were away, driving through the cold
darkness that had not yet become morning.

None of the familiar landscape could be seen, just
sometimes the shape of tree or hill against the sky.
Swans could have been taking off from a lagoon, or an
egret standing in the cold water: ducks could have been
asleep with their heads under their wings, but the
charged darkness hid everything.

The twins asked for a stop when they were deep in
the forest so that they could smell the bush at night.
Then they went on, rattling and bumping on the
narrow earth road through the trees.

Grey light was filtering down when they reached
Back Creek.

Suddenly they saw them—great grey shadows,
great curved shadows, flowing, bounding through the
bush.

'Oh, look!' gasped Sally, and Joanna slowed up.
The headlights shone on a shape sitting poised in the
centre of the road, paws held up in supplication.

David's voice was tense.

'Kangaroos!' he whispered.

The one on the road, dazzled by the headlights, sat
perfectly still; then, as Joanna switched the lights off,
they saw him hop away into the bush and join the per-
petually moving frieze through the peppermints and
wattle scrub; the leaping, bounding, curved, graceful

kangaroos, who were just solid shadows in the shadowy bush night.

'What smooth and lovely movement,' said Joanna.

'Just look,' said Alex. 'There are about ten of them grazing on the little flat beyond the creek—all sizes.'

Joanna leant forward over the wheel, peering through the faint light. 'Oh, there are some quite young ones!' she exclaimed.

The twins sat gripping the bar over the dashboard, gazing at the kangaroos. Then, as they watched, the grazing mob began to leap, without hurrying, towards the Snowy Mountain Authority camp. They leapt slowly, a miracle rhythm of tails, feet, strong hind legs and small balancing forepaws.

Joanna took her foot off the brake, and let the Land Rover roll on, following the wonderful mob of shadow kangaroos towards the camp.

'The Major has always told me that they hop among the tents,' Alex muttered, 'but I hardly visualized this!'

'Make an Australian Bush Ballet,' whispered Joanna.

'They're looking for salt around the tents,' Alex said. 'I think the Major puts it out for them.'

The kangaroos hopped in among the tents for a few moments and then finally melted off into the bush.

'There's smoke going up from the main hut. Someone's awake,' David said.

'We must report that we're going up, so that's a good thing,' his father answered. But they sat with the engine still running, watching the last of the kangaroos bound away.

'I wonder where they go?' David murmured.

'No caves about here that I know of,' said Joanna, 'if you're thinking of the Dragon-fly Cave. But we could ask.'

When they reached the door of the main building the Major was standing on the step, a younger man beside him.

'Admiring our kangaroos?' he laughed.

Joanna and Alex spoke together.

'Yes, we are. Aren't they beautiful!'

'Going ski-ing?' the Major asked, looking at the ski-tips that hung out of the Rover. 'There's plenty of snow.' Then he introduced the younger man, Professor Bisley. 'He was coming to see you today, so you've saved him a trip.'

Alex Dane shook hands with the stranger, looking at him with a slightly questioning expression, knowing that he had neither met him nor heard of him before.

Professor Bisley was English.

'I'm on exchange at Sydney University,' he explained. 'Anthropology, and I was stupid enough not to realize that I'd be running into snow at this time of year if I came up here to look at the brolga and moth aborigine drawings that your children found. I got over the Gap all right, but I can't ski, so I won't be able to get to the cave.'

Alex Dane smiled at him.

'What bad luck,' he said. 'Most years, at this time, you would have found far less snow.'

David had been listening eagerly and now he spoke.

'Do you know if there are any other caves near here, ones with dragon-flies drawn on them?'

Alex Dane put his hand on David's shoulder.

'We've heard of a Dragon-fly Cave,' he explained, 'and that many kangaroos go near it. After seeing these kangaroos David was just wondering. . . .'

'I haven't heard of any other caves or drawings near here,' Bisley answered slowly, 'but I have heard mention of some dragon-fly drawings somewhere between the Mitta Mitta and the Murray. I didn't hear where the cave actually is.'

'I've heard of that cave,' the Major said. 'I've got a young chap among my surveyors whose people have lived over near Tallangatta for generations, and he mentioned some aboriginal drawings somewhere up there.'

'Of *course*! There are lots of kangaroos there,' said David, his face quite stiff with excitement.

'Would your young fellow be about for us to ask?' Alex Dane turned to the Major.

'I'm afraid he's away for a day or so; due back tomorrow, I think,' the Major answered. 'I'll just see.' He went back into the hut and returned, saying: 'You might see him. His mate tells me he intended to spend a couple of nights at Dead Horse hut ski-ing.'

'Oh, good!' said Sally, who had been standing very quietly.

'You might have to go some, to catch him, young lady,' the Major laughed.

'He's fast, is he?' asked Joanna, smiling.

'Oh, he'll be way up at the top of the Ramshead soon after dawn, but you'll see his tracks. You and your husband would have no trouble catching him downhill, but the young fry would have to move!'

After a minute or so more of talking there in the thin, early light, the Danes were on their way—towards the Geehi Wall and the great mountains, towards the snow, the white highway whose magic had already begun to cast a spell over the twins, and towards possible tidings of the Dragon-fly Cave.

Dawn came, lighting up the shadowy bush. No longer was there a moving frieze of shadow kangaroos: instead there was the immense sweep of the Alps, glittering in snow—the white dome of Twynam, the fairy-castle rocks of Watson's Crags, the great spur of Townsend where skis could run so fast, swinging down and down towards Geehi.

    ★   ★   ★   ★   ★

There was some snow in the mountain ash forests, up from Little Mick, clinging in rosettes to the bark of the mountain ash trees, coating logs and lying at the feet of the immense trees. Thick, soft snow bowed down the snowgums when they drove up a little higher, and snow was cold and white on the road. At Dead Horse Gap the glint and sparkle of powder snow covered all the land.

Joanna flung open her door and leapt out, taking a deep, cold breath.

'This is magnificent,' she said. 'Jump out, twins!'

'Boots on, skis on,' chanted their father, 'and away we go!' He looked with longing up to the birthday-cake top of the Ramshead, but the twins were not strong enough to get all the way up there yet.

No smoke came from the chimney of the hut, so the young surveyor had left early.

'I'll go and see if he really did camp here,' Alex said, as he pulled skis out of the back of the Rover.

Joanna smiled.

'See where his tracks go, too. We'll be ski-ing on that side of the road, anyway, so let's carry these across.' She stood in her dark grey ski trousers and blue jacket holding a pair of skis resting on their tips, upright, beside her. 'Three or four miles down there is where they are building the new ski village, and the chair lift is to start this season.'

They crossed the road on the Crackenback fall of the Gap, and went a little way down; then they put on their skis with the cold snow sticking to the steel edges, biting their fingers.

'It looks like a thousand million diamonds,' Sally said. 'We have never seen it like this, powdery and freezing cold.'

'It feels lovely under your skis,' said David, leaning his weight on his ski-sticks, and sliding his feet back and forth. 'It is light.'

'Fast, I should think,' Sally laughed.

'Yes,' said Joanna. 'It will be fast. Your ski-track will be like a matt-surface ribbon on the glittering snow, and the powder may fly up round your shins.'

'And if you make good turns,' said Alex's laughing voice, 'snow spume will fly all round you.'

'Hello, Daddy! Did he spend the night here?'

'Someone did, and whoever it was has gone across this slope a little higher up.'

L

'Well, he must have crossed the creek,' Joanna said, 'and climbed that beautiful spur on the other side, because I can see one single spoor of someone climbing with seal skins on their skis.'

Alex looked up to where she was pointing. A lovely slope with very few trees on it led up towards one of the Ramshead peaks.

'You're right,' he said. 'I can see the track on this side of it, but I can't see any sign of the climber.'

'Let's follow his track and go over there,' Joanna said. 'I should think he is sure to come back down that same spur.'

The twins found themselves following their mother up the slope and then on a long traverse through bushes and small snowgums, and the track on which they travelled was the track made by the young surveyor who might know something of the Dragon-fly Cave. David slid his skis in long, gliding steps behind Sally's skis, and she slid hers behind their mother's— left ski, right ski, right stick, left stick, push and glide, push and glide, roll along over the snow. He could actually feel his father moving behind him too, a powerful rhythm holding them all as each one simultaneously moved across the snow slope of the white ribbon track.

David kept wondering about this man who had made the track. Would he really know about the Dragon-fly Cave? It seemed somehow unlikely that anyone would be able to give them more than a hint of how to find it, but the man had entered into his imagination as sun- and snow-bronzed, hawk-faced, flying down the slope, his skis hidden in a froth of snow, bearing old tales of a kangaroo road through the bush, of rocks, and a forgotten cave.

The track up the opposite slope was too steep for them to follow without seal skins to stop their skis slipping, so they traversed back and forth across it, climbing higher and higher with each traverse.

When they stopped for a rest, David said:

'How are we going to manage to ski down in the deep snow?'

'Fly like a thrush or a rainbow bird, swooping and diving,' Joanna answered with a chuckle.

Alex laughed

'*Not* the piercing flight of a kingfisher, please. You might not stop till you hit the Crackenback!'

'Don't let's worry how we're going to get down,' said Sally, laughing too.

From where they stood they could see right up to the Ramshead, and suddenly Joanna pointed high up.

'Isn't that someone moving—just coming out of those rocks?'

'Yes, it is,' answered Sally.

Far away up the slope a small figure was emerging from the rocks, coming downwards, no bigger than a moth—or a dragon-fly.

They stood still watching, and David gazed up the slope with that odd feeling that a dream was coming true, that this man would be burnt bronze and wild-faced. Already he came like a hawk diving. What word would he bring?

Down he was coming, down, down, no longer the

size of a moth, but taking the form of a man or a bird, and he swung down the steep white slope, hawk or dollar bird, swinging down the sky.

The twins watched and wondered. Joanna and Alex Dane watched and felt each movement of the skier in their own bodies, as they had felt it so often, years before.

They were standing where the ridge flattened for a short way before dropping steeply to the confluence of three creeks that made the Crackenback River.

'He may stop here before he goes on down. I don't think we'll spoil his run,' Joanna said.

He came down straight, streaking through space, feet together, knees together and slightly bent. As the ridge flattened his speed dropped, then he saw them and christied to a stop on a little bump right beside them. Snow frothed up all around.

David was tense with excitement. The skier was bronzed, was hawk-faced, seemed like a winged god of the mountains, just as he had imagined.

Alex suddenly realized they did not know his name.

'Hello!' he said. 'The Major told us we would find one of his surveyors here. Are you . . . ?'

'I am,' the deep blue eyes were laughing and he looked from Alex to Joanna and on to the twins. 'You must be the Danes. My name is Tony Bell.'

Alex looked at the keen-faced man framed by the glittering snow.

'There is a professor of anthropology at the camp who has come to see aborigine rock drawings,' he said, 'and the Major mentioned that you knew the where-abouts of the cave with dragon-fly drawings, somewhere between the Murray and the Mitta, across from Walwa.'

'Well, I do and I don't,' said Mr. Bell. 'I know it's there, but I don't know exactly where'; then he saw David's face and he spoke directly to him. 'I heard about the drawings you found up here in the summer, are you very keen to find some more?'

David nodded and murmured, 'Yes.'

'But how did you first hear of this other cave? As far as I know, very few people know it exists.'

David and Sally looked at their parents uneasily, and Joanna caught their eyes even through the masking dark glasses, and smiled.

'It seems to be an old aborigine tale,' she said. 'We have heard of it from time to time, and one old man over at Kiandra told the twins that is where the kangaroos go.'

'Yes, I believe that's right,' the young man said, and David saw him looking with far-seeing eyes, way down the Crackenback to the blue Monaro. 'My grandfather knew where it was, but as far as I could understand from him, it was a close secret of just a few aborigines. He believed it was the cave of some very important initiates.' He paused and it was as though he had said all he was going to say.

Joanna let her skis sideslip softly on the snow.

'What sort of initiates?' she asked.

Tony Bell smiled.

'My grandfather used to tell me that they were men whose spirits, the aborigines believed, had been on the earth several times, each time surviving hardships to get stronger, and each time becoming more deeply part of the whole land so that they knew the birds and the animals and the growing things, the winds, the floods and the seasons more intimately than even the great men of the tribe. I think that is perhaps why he never told me exactly where it was.' He picked up a small handful of snow and tossed it, shining, into the air. 'Those particular initiates, after passing through many strange experiences, and learning to have courage and wisdom, had to find their own way there, following the kangaroos, listening to the words in the wind. Once they found it, the secrets of the bush were theirs for ever. That is the story according to my grandfather.'

'I see,' said Joanna, her voice blending with the mountain breeze.

David's voice was hardly louder as he spoke at the same time:

'Then it must come after the Brolga Moon and the flood. It may be ages before we find it—if we ever do.'

Mr. Bell had jumped his skis round, pointing downhill, and was holding himself poised on his sticks, but he heard at least part of what David murmured, and gave him a curious glance before he said to Joanna and Alex:

'Join me in my run down to the bottom.'

Joanna looked doubtfully at the twins.

'The children will get down somehow. If they want to find the Dragon-fly Cave they will have to be able to surmount all difficulties,' and he laughed at them and said: 'Just follow without spoiling this wonderful snow. Come on!' he said; and then the three of them had taken

off like birds through the air and with the same per-
fection.

The twins, afraid to wait a moment in case the
powerful magnetism of their flying figures was
weakened, pointed their own skis downwards on the
slope of beautiful snow to follow the three leaders—
to dance downwards in snow spume.

For a while it seemed as if the powdered diamond
snow, or the bright day—or perhaps the hawk-faced
skier—had cast a spell over them. Perhaps the rhythm
of the closely followed three entered into them,
because the twins, too, went flying down the slope.
They went straight at first, with the snow bubbling
and frothing round their knees, then swinging towards
the valley, then a long turn above rocks.

It was magic, completely magic, Sally thought. She
could feel the rush of air through her hair, against her
face. She leant on the air and knew the meaning of
speed. She had heard her mother and father so often
say: 'Relax! Bend your knees. Lean out. Relax!' Now
she relaxed and felt her knees and ankles absorb any
bumps, felt the skis slide faster, faster through the snow.

One could not, however, be magic all the time, and
suddenly Sally was buried, face first, in the deep cold
snow, her mouth full of it, her eyes full of it, her ears
and nose full of it. She dug herself out, and tried to
brush the thick snow off her windcheater and dark
blue trousers. Another snow-covered heap shook itself
beside her, and David emerged. The spell had broken
for them both, and the other three skiers were at the
foot of the slope looking up.

'Now we must go on without them to follow,' said David, laughing. 'And I think we'll find we are not such wonderful skiers after all.'

'Follow their tracks. Try and get the same feeling again,' suggested Sally, but in a few moment she was buried once more.

They tumbled and crashed their way down to the others, but just for an occasional brief second they found that feeling again, the feeling of flying through a world that is only composed of snow and air. At the bottom the hawk-faced surveyor said:

'Well done. You are triers all right.' Then he looked at them half gravely, half laughing. 'You will have to know far more of the secrets of the snow before you reach the Dragon-fly Cave, but I will draw you a sketch map and show you where I think the cave may be, and where you must leave the road and take to the bush. I have searched and never found it, but I'm pretty certain where it is. You may have the eyes to see it.' He had taken his dark glasses off for a moment, and now he put them on again, and there were no half-laughing eyes for the twins to see, only the reflection, in each lens, of the Ramshead Range, like fairy castles iced with powder snow, and David thought of Black Mag, above the stream, at Waterfall Farm, pointing towards the mountains. Here in the southern end of the Alps they had been told some of the secrets of the Dragon-fly Cave.

16 : Brolga Moon

'WELL, I'm blowed if I can see anything wrong with it.' Alex Dane's voice was exasperated as he looked round the side of the Land Rover bonnet at Joanna in the driving seat. 'Give her another go.'

Joanna pressed the self-starter again and there was only an unenthusiastic whirr. She felt the afternoon cold creeping round them.

'I think it would be better for the twins to put on their boots again and ski till we get her going,' she said.

They had already pushed the Land Rover off the top of the Gap so that it ran downhill, but the engine had not started. Now they were in a deeply snowed little valley where a creek ran under the turn on the road.

The twins pulled off their desert boots, put their ski-boots on again and got out their skis and sticks. They were tired and they moved slowly across the deep powder snow.

'This is even fluffier,' said Sally, flicking some up on the basket of her ski-stick.

'Gets less sun here and probably not a whisper of wind,' David said thoughtfully, looking down the little gully that opened into the wide valley of the Dead Horse Creek. 'It will take us years and years to learn the secrets of the snow. It seems as if the Dragon-fly Cave is found only by people who know *all* the secrets of our world, so we may never find it, and yet I certainly thought that Black Mag meant that if we did get there it would be fairly soon.'

'I don't think she meant that we had to know every-thing,' said Sally. 'I think she just did not know if we would get through all the things that were going to happen to us, and unless we got through them all right we'd never find the Dragon-fly Cave.' She slid her long skis slowly forward through the snow. 'After all, we've found the kingfisher feathers to guard us and bring us luck.'

'There's still the Brolga Moon and the flood,' muttered David.

Suddenly Joanna joined them on her skis.

'Daddy's going to stay by the Rover and see what he can do till someone comes along,' she said. 'Come on, follow me!' and she set off in a series of dancing turns from side to side of the gully, with the snow flying up high.

Down at the entrance to the main valley Sally found her skis unexpectedly shoot forward as she went under the outer branches of a large tree. She gasped as she only just managed to stop falling backwards.

'Feels as if there's ice there, Mummy,' she said, as she slowed to a stop beside Joanna.

'Pieces of frozen snow that have fallen off the leaves,' Joanna explained. 'Sometimes the snow is crusty under the trees. You will learn,' she laughed and looked at the snowy twins. She, too, was wondering about the Dragon-fly Cave . . . and wondering whether, if they found it, it might not perhaps be a disappointing ending to all their wonderful adventures. But she realized, which the twins perhaps did not, that every test foretold by Black Mag, everything that had happened since that hot New Year's Day at the bridge where the Murray starts, had made the twins more deeply aware of all that was around them—more deeply part of the whole land, just as the young surveyor had said of the aborigines who found the Dragon-fly Cave. The secrets of the bush were theirs for ever, he had said. Joanna looked at the snowgums and the evening light falling over the snow and for a moment the bush was hers because she loved it so deeply.

It was a long time before they heard the sound of a truck coming over Dead Horse Gap from the Crackenback, and in all that time Alex Dane had been completely unable to see why the Land Rover would not go. When the truck driver got out to help, he could find nothing wrong either.

The twins were getting very tired, almost too tired to feel the excitement in being out late in the mountains, the excitement in the long, violet-blue shadows on the snow and the mysterious blue wells of shadow in the valleys below. Joanna was beginning to look worried. Then all of a sudden Alex pressed the self-starter and the engine gave a roar.

'Well!' he said. 'There seemed no earthly reason why it wouldn't go, and no reason now for it to start. Anyway, I'll keep it going.' He turned to the truck driver to thank him and the man merely waved his hand and said:

'You go ahead. I'll push from behind if you stick again. There's plenty of downhill, anyway!'

Thus it was that they left the snow late in the evening, though they had intended to go by three in the afternoon.

Light was still pale in the sky around the snow when they drove up through the gloom on the Geehi Wall. Night fell before they reached the Back Creek, and only their headlights pierced the heavy darkness of the bush. They could see the bright stars shining in the sky when they drove out into the Swampy Plains Valley, and just as they were passing the sleeping paddocks of the Adamses' station the full moon rose up the sky.

'What a huge moon!' Sally said, peering across her father to see it. Then she became tense. 'Very soon we come to the reserve where there are often brolgas.'

Joanna felt herself becoming taut, too. She had had a queer feeling all the latter part of the afternoon that something was holding them back in the mountains. Now it seemed as though it was intended that they should be travelling home in the night . . . by the light of the full moon.

The moon appeared to shoot up the sky, filling the valley with cold, pale light and dense shadows.

Unconsciously Alex Dane had slowed up the Land Rover as they approached the turn in the road by the reserve. Though he had not seen Black Mag when she appeared at the bridge, he had seen her on the cliff above the river, and seen the strange men on horseback on the Yellow Bog. He had seen the aborigine stockman who had such unusual knowledge of the twins' whereabouts when they were lost on 'the tops', and he had realized that many of the old lubra's prophecies had come true. Now he was wondering about the Brolga Moon. He felt a cold shiver of apprehension. Black Mag had said that she had seen the twins in the roaring waters of the flood but that she had *never* seen them at the Dragon-fly Cave. Were the waters of the flood the one test which they would not get through? He turned the Rover round the sharp corner.

'Look!' David whispered. 'Four brolgas, and they're dancing in the moonlight!'

'I'll keep the Land Rover just ticking over,' his father murmured, and he turned it slightly so that they could all see the stately, beautiful dance of the four immense birds.

Moonlight made their lovely grey colour shimmer and change from pale to dark. They stepped and bowed, parted, spread their wings and advanced towards each other, stepped and bowed, and parted again, dancing in a ghostly rhythm on the moon-blanched grass.

The two male birds bowed before their mates and both bent their long necks, put their heads to the ground, and picked up small sticks which they threw in the air with a graceful flick of their necks, caught them, advanced, bowed, threw their sticks, spread their wings, sprang in the air, back and forth, dancing in the moonlight.

David and Sally, watching breathlessly through the windscreen, felt they could sit still no longer. The dance drew them irresistibly. They did not even feel surprised when, as though someone had told them to, their mother and father both opened the doors and slid quietly out into the cold moonlight.

It was then that Sally began to feel as if all the forest on the far side of the reserve was full of moving shadows and faint sounds. The frost-dried redgrass, where the brolgas danced, was bleached by the light of the moon, but the dark forest stood not far away, hiding all manner of things—the animals and birds that lived there, and the dreams and memories that had come creeping in by the light of the Brolga Moon.

She saw a mopoke like a small grey ghost on a bough, but it was the moving dark shadows, which she may or may not have seen, that filled her with unrest.

'I'm going to get closer by going up the creek bed,' she whispered, barely realizing that it was not only the brolgas to which she wished to be closer. David followed her.

The creek bed was filled with moonlight for the first hundred yards, and they crept along, only occasionally peering over the top at the dancing birds. Once the tremendous span of a pair of outspread wings obscured the moon. Then, where the creek turned parallel with the forest, its deep bed was in shadow. At the turn into the darkness Sally hesitated, then something drew her on, one foot after another, into the shadow. They were very close to the brolgas. A few steps further, and the shadow of the forest lay out across the grass, beyond the creek bed.

It was then that Sally began to feel really afraid— but she was not afraid of anything she could actually see or hear. The thought went racing through her: 'If I go into the shadows, I will never ever be able to find the Dragon-fly Cave.' Then she felt David's hand on her arm, and he was trembling.

There was no real sound in the forest except the cry of the mopoke, yet they felt that there was the weaving movement of the darkness going on at the same time as the brolgas' dance in the light.

Sally stood quite still, and David beside her, still except for their trembling, and the strangest thing of all was that they felt as if they were being drawn by invisible hands and soundless voices. Then Sally knew that she must choose between the shadows and the dance in the light. Just at that moment she heard a rustle in the creek bed, the unmistakable, slithery rustle of a snake. A coil brushed up against her leg and passed her. There were snakes in the darkness.

Simultaneously Sally and David sprang up the creek bank into the moonlight, leaving the snake and the soundless, invisible shadows behind them.

They were right beside the brolgas, but the birds were so intent on their dance that they took no notice of them. Joanna had come along the creek as soon as she saw the twins go into the shadow, and was standing as still as a tree on the bank, but the birds took no notice of anything. They never even looked at the twins as they crept slowly along to meet their mother through the moon-drenched light. Sally wanted to run with joy, as if they had avoided some untold danger that lurked in the dark forest, and she was longing to dance with the brolgas, to step and bow, to have wings to spread.

Then, without any warning, the brolgas began to utter their screeving call, and, one after the other, they took off with slowly beating wings and feet outstretched behind. In slow circles they rose, calling to the moon. The twins stood beside their mother, watching the great birds circle up and up into the deep night sky, silhouetted against the moon. Just as Alex joined them they heard the sound which must have disturbed the brolgas: the sound of a shod horse, and the rattle of a sulky's wheels.

17 : The road was empty

THAT DAY at the Adamses' homestead had been very cheerful. Rickie and Margaret had arrived home from school the night before and most of the day had passed happily, playing with the younger children, the cats and dogs, and riding their ponies. Jane Adams had been delighted. It was so lovely to have the children home, and Rickie was so much less superior, so much readier to talk.

Jane had gone out for a ride with them, and it was then that she realized that Rickie was more inclined to talk. While Margie had cantered ahead, Rickie had mentioned something about which he had apparently been thinking a good deal.

'Mummy,' he said as he sat on his bay pony, 'do you think if I tried to learn all I could about the birds, and the bush and, oh, everything, I might get as much fun as David and Sally do?'

Jane looked at him, startled, but she knew that she, too, had been thinking that the twins had got a double share of that special quality of the Danes which she herself had never been able to understand.

'They do find a lot of fun in life, don't they?' she said. 'Uncle Alex and Aunt Joanna always have too,' and she thought of the excitement that Joanna got from the sight of a kingfisher flying, or the song of a white-throated warbler.

'Yes,' said Rickie, 'they do. They seem to see everything quite differently from the way anyone else does. Different things seem more important to them.' He looked at his mother with a puzzled grin. 'Then when you stop to think, the things that are important to them often *are* important.'

'You've been stopping and thinking a good deal,' said Jane.

'Yes, but all the same, sometimes the whole Dane family do seem to be a bit crazy.'

'I know,' said Jane, 'but when you understand what they're doing, it's got some sense in it.'

'Well, that mad dash for the kingfisher feather, last holidays,' Rickie muttered, 'and yet they were so happy when they'd got it. . . .'

Jane laughed.

'That's just it. They seem to get more joy out of life than anyone else I know.'

'It would be interesting to know how or why,' Rickie said wistfully, and Jane sighed because it seemed to her that Rickie was on a hopeless quest.

'Would you mind if I rode up to the reserve at moonrise tonight, to see if the brolgas are there?' he asked. 'The twins have been murmuring things about brolgas dancing by moonlight. . . .'

'That will be all right if you promise not to be too long,' Jane answered. 'The Danes themselves appear to be on some sort of search at present—for brolgas by moonlight and kingfisher feathers, and aborigine drawings,' she said, and thought to herself that Rickie could hardly fail to find pleasure and contentment in trying to learn about the bush birds and animals.

When Rickie went out to get his pony that night she had slipped her halter and was grazing some distance off. The moon rose just when he had caught her, and he had five or ten minutes' ride to the reserve—five or ten minutes' ride alone in the frosty moonlight.

He heard a stationary car engine purring, before he saw the tail-light of the Land Rover, and he slowed up his pony and made sure he walked on the grass edge of the road. For a moment Rickie felt that he did not really care about brolgas and that because his pony had slipped her halter he had already been longer away than his mother expected and it would be better to go back, then he rode on slowly—more curious about the car than the birds. It did not occur to him that there was anyone else watching the brolgas till he saw the Land Rover and thought it belonged to the Danes. Just then the brolgas started crying out to the moon and rising in their great, slow circles, and Rickie saw the Dane family in their ski clothes, walking hurriedly, it seemed, across the reserve to the road. Except for the Land Rover, the road was an empty white ribbon stretching both ways.

Rickie let himself through the big boundary gate by the mail box. He heard David's voice say: '*That's* only Rickie,' and wondered whom they had expected to see. Obviously the twins expected someone because they stopped and peered up and down the road, staring for a long time at the trees down by the culvert.

'Hullo, Rickie,' everyone said at once. 'Didn't expect to see you out at this time.' And then Alex Dane said:

'You didn't happen to see or hear a sulky going by, did you?' He knew someone must ask, and this time he had heard it clearly himself. As he spoke the shadows of the brolgas passed over them while the huge birds flew under the moon.

'A sulky!' Rickie was really surprised. 'I've only ever seen one or two on the road! No, not a sight or sound of one.'

Joanna switched off the Land Rover engine.

'I didn't turn it off before because of the birds,' she explained, then David's urgent voice broke the silence.

'I can still hear it faintly—down by the culvert— can't you?'

They all listened and it seemed as if the Danes were almost hanging on Rickie's reply.

'Can't hear a thing,' he said regretfully.

Joanna could hear it, and yet she did not say so, because of Rickie, but Sally pulled David by the hand.

'Come on, let's try to find her. Quick!' she said, and before their parents could stop them, the two children had scrambled through the fence to cut a corner down to the little patch of trees.

'Better turn the Land Rover and go down too,' Joanna said.

'I'll follow,' said Rickie, puzzled almost beyond speech.

From high above came the brolgas' cry. Rickie could hear no other sound. The twins heard the brolgas, and very faintly they could still hear the clip, clop, clip, clop, and the rattle of wheels.

Forgetting all else, Sally and David ran and ran.

They ran with feet thudding, hearts pounding, ears listening for the sound of the sulky, and eyes strained for the sight of it, strained to see through the moonlight and shadow, the white and black of the hour. The cold air bit into their flesh, went through their hair like ice and hurt their bursting lungs.

There was a sudden prolonged calling from the brolgas, circling in the sky, and the sound of the sulky vanished completely. The road beyond the trees was undoubtedly empty, yet they had heard those wheels there, in the trees. Perhaps Black Mag had pulled up in their shadow. The twins ran on. They heard the Land Rover turning round and then coming down the road, but they reached the trees a second or so ahead.

On the fringe of the trees they stopped quite still. The road was empty, empty of everything except faint horse- and wheel-tracks that faded away, but it was as if the whole grove of gum trees and the cold air in the hollow were whispering.

The children stood tingling all over, and then they both thought they heard Black Mag's voice come in the whisper of the gum leaves: 'Wisdom is given in the light of the Brolga Moon, and the kingfisher feather guards from danger.'

Sally was doing a little dance, like a willy-willy, in the centre of the white road, as the Land Rover pulled up, but she had stopped when Rickie arrived. Joanna and Alex got out of the Rover, both listening as though they, too, heard something in the breeze and the whisper of the leaves. Then Rickie arrived and Alex said:

'No sulky! We must have imagined it.' He looked at Rickie with a smile and added: 'The Danes being mad again! But we have seen a sulky going about the place a few times just lately.'

'Don't you feel that we *must* reach the Dragon-fly Cave now?' Sally murmured to David.

'Yes,' he whispered back, and they were both so excited that they never once thought of the sombre roar of the flood.

18 : Entering into the mystery

'IT'S NO USE searching for the Dragon-fly Cave yet,' Sally said, 'not 'til we've been through every test that Black Mag mentioned.'

'Yes, I suppose you're right.' David sat thinking for a while, then said: 'I wonder when Mummy and Daddy will take us ski-ing again? Even if the Dragon-fly Cave is not up in the high mountains, ski-ing is more exciting than anything I've ever done. Just when we really seemed to be getting it, that time following the surveyor, it was even more wonderful than galloping after a beast.'

Sally nodded.

'Yes, much more.'

'She must have meant something, when she pointed to the mountains,' David said, thinking back to Black Mag's ghost-like visitation to Waterfall Farm.

'Well, we did get all that information from Mr. Bell in the mountains.'

'Yes, but I think there's something else. Perhaps there's a test up there, but perhaps it is only that we must learn.' Suddenly he turned to her eagerly. 'Don't you feel, when you're really getting near it—like the start of that run in powder snow that day—that in a second you'll learn some wonderful secret?'

'Yes, something like that—or perhaps that you've been made into someone else. Whatever it is, it is marvellous.'

A lot more snow had fallen on the Alps since the day the Danes had met the surveyor, Bell, and they had been ski-ing at Dead Horse Gap quite often. They even took Rickie and Margie once, and the twins' ski-ing had improved a great deal. Now the school holidays were over and the Adamses had gone back, the real winter was closing in, but the Danes were thinking more and more of snow and ski technique, and distances they could travel. It was as though they had another challenge, the challenge of the mountains, the challenge to get themselves strong enough to travel long distances over the snow, the challenge to become good skiers so that they could ski down really steep slopes and not leave them spoiled by ragged tracks.

Life seemed altogether challenging but altogether marvellous.

It was their mother and father who made the suggestion that gave the winter its absolute finishing touch of glory.

They had finished dinner one night when the wind was crying round the house and there was bitter cold outside. The log fire burnt hot and slow, a yellowbox back log not crumbling, not breaking, simply keeping its own red-hot shape. The twins were half asleep on the sofa. Alex and Joanna were in deep chairs on either side.

'Well,' said Alex, 'shall we tell them our plan?'

Sally and David looked a little wider awake.

Joanna smiled and nodded.

'How would you like to spend a couple of weeks at Thredbo, the ski village they are building down the Crackenback River, not far from Dead Horse Gap?' Alex asked.

Something made that instant remain as a picture and a sound in Sally's mind for a long time. The red fire and the wild night outside, her father's voice calling up pictures of the great, glittering white mountains that had been invisible for days of blizzard weather. The twins were no longer sleepy, they were sitting up clasping their knees, faces glowing, eyes very bright.

That was the start of it. When Alex got word that the road was sufficiently cleared for four-wheel-drive vehicles to get over the mountains, they loaded their clothes and skis into the Land Rover and set forth, leaving their valley for the wet bush and then the snow-laden forests, mysterious and magnetic.

They skied at Dead Horse Gap during the middle part of the day, and the untracked snow was even colder, even lighter, now, at the end of June, than it had been the day they had skied there with the surveyor, Bell.

David climbed quite a long way up on his own and when he stopped to get his breath he looked with longing up at the Ramshead. No rock showed black, the entire peak was white and drawn over with blue shadows, shining white against the blue sky. There alone, high above the others, he realized the profound silence of the winter mountains. He saw how deeply the light penetrated the snow and how the many facets of the snow crystals reflected the golden sun and the blue sky. All the mountain world that he knew in summer was hidden beneath this beautiful snow, transformed into what he suddenly knew to be an almost magic world, a world of hidden secrets, of great adventures, a world of great happiness, and—he knew—a world that could hold great danger.

Now he had to try to ski down the softly glittering slope without spoiling it—make his tracks as beautiful as he possibly could.

The day was so happy that it was like a dream—and, still dreaming, they drove down to Thredbo late in the afternoon, to the collection of little houses on one side of the Crackenback River, and the lovely steep mountains on the other side, with a chair lift going up Crackenback Peak.

The twins looked at the ski-trails cut down through the trees, at the little figures of a few late skiers coming down. The profound quietness of a calm, cold winter evening was already enfolding the opposite slope, only the peaks still flared with light. The mountains, in spite of the pylons and chair lift, in spite of the few skiers, were withdrawing into their essential remoteness.

Joanna looked up too, as they got out of the Land Rover, and then back to the twins.

'This is the place to learn to ski,' she said, and a voice beside them answered:

'It certainly is. Did you twins take me seriously when I said you would have to know the secrets of the snow?' There was Mr. Bell, the hawk-faced surveyor.

'Hullo!' said Joanna and Alex. David and Sally smiled, and felt a sudden pulse of excitement beating.

Mr. Bell was interested in the Danes because he himself had never heard any old aborigine tales around the district about the Dragon-fly Cave, he had only heard of it from his father. In fact, there were very few people left who knew the aborigines. He had been pondering how the Danes really did know of it.

'You won't be ski-ing in the ski school all day,' he said, smiling at the twins, 'so we will have some runs together. I am here for a week, and will be back again for the following weekend.'

Alex found out days later that Tony Bell had asked the ski instructors, who were friends of his, to teach the twins as much snowcraft as possible. As there were not many skiers there at the beginning of the season, this had been possible, and the whole Dane family found themselves having a most wonderful time.

The twins were excited to find that the instructors

made ski-ing seem more easy, and that they had both reached a stage of ski-ing and of fitness in which they could make their limbs do as they wished them to do. Their ski-ing improved quickly. They spent hours each morning and afternoon following a cheerful boy called Otto, who not only showed them how to ski, but taught them about snow and mountains. He taught them to watch for the patches where a dull surface on the snow told that it had been touched by wind and was sticky, slower or perhaps crusty. He taught them how snow changed beneath trees after a snowfall had been over for some time, how sun changed it, and frost. He taught them to watch for ice, and because they were so eager to learn they had great fun together.

'You do well, David,' Otto said, as David came dancing down to him. 'Now, Sally,' he called, and down Sally came, feet together, knees together.

It was their last weekend. Fresh snow had fallen overnight and there was untracked powder all over the south face of the mountains. Tony Bell had arrived back. Now they could see him coming towards them.

'Come on!' said Otto. 'Show Tony how much you have improved. Follow close to me this time, David and then Sally.'

Otto waved to Tony Bell, then pointed his skis downwards. The twins followed him. For some reason it mattered very much to them to be able to ski as perfectly as possible for Tony Bell to see. It was as though he, too, were judging them.

When Otto did a quick sideslip to check, David checked too, put in his stick, made the same little jump

as Otto, pushed out gently with his heels in the long
gliding turn, down, down the slope, standing up on his
skis, going fast yet in control, snow spume flying. This
was it: this was ski-ing, the skis running softly, smoothly
through the snow: this was the magic, the entering into
the mystery.

Behind him, making a third set of tracks beside his
and Otto's, came Sally, the cold air blowing her hair
back, ski-ing with joy.

Tony Bell was close to them as they came to Lovers'
Leap, a good steep pitch, and untracked so far.

Otto did not stop. He had somehow got the idea
from Tony that these twins had to prove they possessed
courage, had to learn to ski well, so that in every way
their dealings with the mountains were perfect. He did
one turn on the brink, two sweeping turns on the
steepness, and then schussed way out on to the flatter
part before stopping.

David and Sally were close behind him. Sally saw
David match his turns to Otto's. She also jumped and
leant her weight right outwards, sideslipped fast
through the frothing snow, jumped and leant far out
again.

They stopped beside Otto, and Tony Bell swished
to a stop beside them, throwing snow up in a cloud.

'Well,' he said, 'looks like you two are getting to
know some of the secrets of the snow! Magnificent!' he
said, his smile embracing Otto as well as the twins.
'Listen! I have a plan for tomorrow. I have asked
Hannes if you may come too, Otto, and he says yes, if
you want to. I thought of going over to the Ramshead

from the top of the lift, and ski-ing down to Dead
Horse Gap.'

'If Hannes says I may, I would love to,' Otto smiled.
'We make a tour, twins! We will go over the mountains together.'

Early in the morning they all went up in the lift.
They all had their lunches packed into bags and fastened
on to their belts. Alex had driven the Land Rover up to
the Gap earlier still, and left it there, and Tony Bell had
driven up in his car and brought him back to the
village.

By the time they had got about half-way to the
Ramshead a wind sprang up, but they were all warm
enough, and from where they were they could not see
the great, angry clouds in the Murray Valley.

They skied in amongst a number of rocky tors, all
the rocks plastered with snow and ice.

David went up close to one of them, peering into
the crevices.

'This is where they came for the bogong moths,' he
said, more to Sally and himself than anyone else, but
Tony Bell overheard and looked curiously at the twins.

'Who came for *what*?' asked Otto.

David was embarrassed, but answered:

'The aborigines . . . for bogong moths.'

'Why?'

David looked at Otto's puzzled face and burst out
laughing.

'They lit fires and roasted them and had great
feasts.'

'It's all very hard to understand really,' said Tony,

'because lots of the places that are called Bogong after the moths are above the treeline and they must have had to carry firewood up.'

'So they must,' said David. 'Even here. The lubras would have carried it, I suppose. I wonder if Black Mag ever came this way?'

Suddenly Sally said:

'We're going to have some bad weather.'

They all looked quickly to the north-west and saw the first ominous black clouds coming over the range.

'You are learning to be observant,' Tony chuckled, 'and to live with the weather.'

'Better move along,' said Otto. 'Come, twins, we will try that two-step I showed you, along this flat piece.'

Sunlight fell on the Ramshead making it stand out against the sudden boil-up of black cloud. The wind picked up the snow and whirled it against them.

'Soon snow will fall too,' Otto said. 'We may not have such a comfortable run down, but this will try out your ski technique.'

David felt excited by the coming wild weather, and full of confidence and strength. He couldn't help chuckling and saying:

'Even Otto likes to see us tested out.'

Otto looked questioningly at the twins.

'Come on,' he said, 'the wind starts to talk in the rocks. It is time to go down from the peaks.'

Otto, Joanna, Alex and Tony Bell—they had all been in the mountains a great deal. Perhaps Joanna and Alex who had spent so much of their earlier life 'on the tops' with cattle knew better than any of them how quickly bad weather could come in the Australian Alps, where there are no high peaks to protect the ski country, but even they were immensely surprised by the sudden blizzard that swept down on them out of the north.

'Follow close,' said Otto. 'Let us hurry while we can see. Tony, will you be the last man, please? Ready? Then quick!'

Down he went, down off the Ramshead towards Dead Horse Gap—quickly while it was possible to see anything at all.

The twins knew that now they would have to ski well and not fall over, not hold up the whole party. They saw Otto make his first turn. They turned too. They had been following Otto for hours of every day during the last two weeks, and now they just did what he did exactly as they had been doing it, and tried to copy his every action. At first they did not realize that he was going faster than usual.

They had made less than half a dozen turns when they were enfolded by the blizzard—the wind-hurled snow and the clouds. Even Otto's tracks vanished. Otto himself was like a ghost ahead, through the lashing curtain of snow. They could hardly see their own skis. The snow beat against them from every direction. The mountainside seemed to be falling away steeply below their feet, the slope was bottomless, sucking them down.

Sally gave a gasp of fear. It took courage to jump and lean right out and have complete confidence to follow Otto. They were frightened to do it, and yet frightened they would lose sight of the snow-shrouded figure ahead.

Otto stopped to make sure they were still close. His face was coated with snow.

'That is good. Follow very close and just have confidence that you can do it.'

A peculiarly strong blast shook even Otto, and Sally was blown over.

'You are too light, Sal!' Otto helped her up. 'Eat more,' he laughed, but he looked at Tony and cocked one eyebrow as he said: 'Come on, Sally, follow me, and all keep close.'

The wind roared and whipped the snow savagely at unprotected faces.

Sally tried to keep her eyes on Otto, but she could see nothing else at all, no mountainside, only the thick air, and in a few moments, with her skis plunging away from her, she was over.

Otto must have had some special sense to know that she had fallen. He stopped and climbed back up in a second.

'Sally, it is quite simple, and great fun, to ski blind. You must go with your skis, and lean out,' he said, and added, because he was beginning to get really worried that even this simple run was going to be dangerous: 'Have faith and courage.' Also he was sure that the twins were involved in something much more real than a game, in which courage meant a great deal.

Sally grinned at him, her snow-caked cheeks almost cracking, and with his words she felt the same elation that David had felt at the top. She *would* have courage, even if she had to gather it up every minute, for every turn!

N

'Come on,' said Otto, who, being the leader, had the really difficult ski-ing to do, and the course-finding in all the blizzard.

Down they went, through the vast stinging curtain of snow.

Sally watched Otto unwaveringly, checked when he did, jumped only a second later than his jump— willed herself to have courage and faith, and descended thrillingly over the invisible snow.

Even Otto fell once, as, ski-ing completely blind, he went over the edge of a wind tunnel, and each of the others fell, some more than once. It was very difficult ski-ing, and yet so exciting to be ski-ing down through such a storm.

They stopped for a rest when they reached the trees and some sheltering rocks, and a flight of black cockatoos must have gone wind-borne overhead, because they could hear them crying.

It was too cold to stop long, and they were soon crossing the flat stretch of the ridge then turning down again on the lovely steep part where the Danes had first met the stranger, Tony Bell. Now none of the beautiful slope could be seen, but the snow was good and there were trees for some of the way, which gave some indication of the gradient.

This time Tony went ahead too, David following him, Sally following Otto, and the two men were jodelling, their voices sometimes ringing out, sometimes muffled by the storm.

The twins felt they were throwing themselves into the clouds with each turn. It was an effort of courage to let the skis slide in a long sweeping turn through the dense, white blizzard, and yet it was so exciting.

There was echoing laughter followed by a jodel as Tony disappeared over an unexpected cornice. Then at last they were down by the creek, hearing the wind roaring through the Gap.

'Now, don't let's fall into this,' said Alex cheerfully, as they stopped close to one open, icicled hole in the creek; and Tony Bell clapped each twin on the shoulder and said:

'Well, this should help you to find the Dragon-fly Cave. I think those who belonged to it lived with nature in a very special sort of way. There are many mysteries in life,' he added, 'that cannot be measured by science or made clear by knowledge. The magic of snow, and ski-ing, and mountains is one of them. Perhaps you are following this magic already.'

There, sheltered by the creek banks, the snow fell like a blessing on faces, on hoods, on gloves, in beautiful star-shaped crystals.

19 : The icy waters of the flood

'IT'S TURNED WARM,' Alex Dane said, standing by the office window and sniffing at the hot darkness. 'I'm sure it can't be snowing—probably buckets of rain up there too.'

Joanna raised her voice against the drumming of the rain on the iron roof: 'There must have been almost another inch since I measured it at five o'clock.'

'I should think so,' Alex nodded.

She walked over and joined him, pressing her forehead against the wire netting as she smelt and listened, and felt the weather.

'Listen!' she said sharply.

Alex put his own face right to the window and pursed his lips.

'It's rained on the snow all right. Sounds like quite a lot of water coming.'

They stood listening to the distant roar which the hubbub of the rain could not overlay. Then the ringing of the telephone pierced the noise of the storm. Alex picked up the receiver and, on the crackling line, he could just hear Jane's voice:

'Brian's come in and says to tell you that a big flood is coming down.'

Alex thanked her, but the line had suddenly gone quiet.

'Rain's been too much for the telephone,' he said. 'That was Jane to warn us that a big flood's on its way.'

'Why are you looking bothered?' Joanna asked.

'Am I?' He grinned at her, then he went on: 'Let's both admit it: here's the first flood since the prophecies of old Black Mag.'

'*If* she ever existed,' Joanna amended.

'I'm sure she did, and so are you,' Alex said, and for a moment his grin faded. 'What's even more important, so are the twins.'

Joanna nodded.

'Well,' Alex went on, 'everything has worked out so far, and some of the prophecies have been rather too exciting while coming true. The twins have got colds now, so we can see they are not out early or late, and during the day either you or I can be sure to be out with them, till the flood goes.'

'That's the best way to manage.' Joanna looked at him gratefully. She had not wanted to seem afraid or fussy. 'We won't appear to be keeping a careful eye on them, as they have already got colds.'

'I'll be glad when the "roaring waters of the flood" are over,' said Alex, 'but all the same, I think life'll seem a little quiet if—or when—the Dragon-fly Cave is found.'

'Yes,' Joanna said thoughtfully. 'I have thought about that a good deal, too.' Once again she said 'Listen!' and the noise of the flood sounded much closer.

Soon the flood reached Tiarri and came roaring round the foot of the hill, roaring through the lagoons. Joanna went to see if the twins had woken. All she could hear in the darkness was their heavy, coldy breathing mingled with the sound of the flood.

Later, Sally woke and, hearing the thundering waters, leant over and shook David gently.

'What is it?' he asked, before he was properly awake, and then raised his head up from the pillow and whistled softly. 'Flood!' he said.

'Yes, flood,' Sally answered. 'I think the time is coming for Black Mag's last test.'

'But I wonder just what it will be?' David said, 'because anyone is a fool, and asking to be drowned, if they really get into a flood.'

'That's true,' said Sally, 'but the old man up in the mountains told us to listen to the sound of the flood.'

*   *   *   *   *

The next day the twins' colds were still heavy and, without seeming to be keeping them within sight because of Black Mag's prophecy, Joanna could honestly say she did not want them to go out till later in the morning when it was warmer, and by then she would be ready to go with them. From the garden they watched the surging brown water go round the foot of the hill, but Joanna called them inside to do their school work and keep warm.

An urgent message necessitated Alex going over to the woolshed, but he had thought out a job for the others which, while taking them into the flooded paddocks, which they would certainly want to see, would give them something to think about to take their minds off the 'roaring waters'.

'After all, we must not keep them inside during a flood,' Joanna had said, 'or we will be backing out of the whole thing, if you see what I mean? And the children will feel that they have failed in Black Mag's test, and will never find the Dragon-fly Cave.'

Of course Alex knew she felt that way herself too— had not she been one of those to whom Black Mag had spoken?—and he wished he could be with them. He kept trying to make himself feel that it was absurd to worry, that Black Mag—*if* she really existed—could not have 'seen' the twins in the flood and that Joanna and Sally and David knew far too much to get caught in flood waters. But he could not drive away the fear that, in the flood, they faced a tremendous danger.

There was no gleam of sunshine when Joanna and the twins set off, down the hill, and a plover was uttering its plaintive cry on the flats. Joanna shivered, but the

twins, even with their snuffly colds, were wild with
excitement. Perhaps today they would earn the prize—
or was it the wisdom?—which would make them
worthy of finding the Dragon-fly Cave.

Joanna had, years ago, before the twins were born,
loved the untamed power of the floods, the great sound
of them round the hill at night—the voice of the melted
snow—telling her of all the hidden gullies in the
mountains and from whence the water came. But ever
since the twins had been big enough to walk about she
had not been able to look at the swift, swirling water
and the logs whirling by without realizing what little
chance a child would have in those fierce torrents.

Today she kept watching Sally and David so that
they could not possibly go too close to the edge, but in
spite of her anxiety she, too, felt that the waters were
drawing her and that she must find out whatever
strange secret they held.

Some of the cattle which they had to count were
close to the main river at a place where the current
swirled out and then back to join the stream.

'This is the snow on which we put our lovely
tracks,' said Joanna, and her voice was rather sad.

'There are logs like young trees, going down,' David
said, as he sat on Buckwong watching the water race by.

'Yes,' said Sally, 'and collections of branches almost
like huge birds' nests.'

The Banjo pawed the wet ground nervously.

'It looks bad.' David moved uneasily. 'Too dirty and
swirling, and too full of branches and stuff.'

Just then Sally felt herself go cold with horror.

Crouching terrified on a great heap of branches and rubbish that was whirling towards them before the current took it back into the main stream was a small ringtail possum.

'Oh, look!' she cried, and before anyone else had really seen it she was off The Banjo and plunging through the shallower water that flowed over the paddocks towards the river itself. The heap of rubbish was going round and round in the small whirlpool made by the flood, and it looked as if she could catch hold of it—except that a yard of deep water lay between the flooded paddocks and the edge of the whirling pool.

David, with more appreciation of the danger, threw off his boots and followed her. Joanna, her breath catching with fear, had flown off her horse, and run into the water without waiting to remove either boots or jacket, but just as Sally, with her stick hooked into the heap of branches, lost her footing and was swept towards the possum, Joanna wriggled herself out of her boots, threw off her coat and plunged in after her.

Sally felt the bitter cold of the water grip her like bands of ice around her head and chest. She had only one idea, and that was to save the possum. She caught at the tangled nest of branches and tried to kick herself back out of the whirlpool, but it pulled her in. Her waterlogged boots were weighing her down. She had no breath, and the river, the great, cold river, was taking her. Then she felt Joanna's hand on her shoulder, and she grabbed the little animal off its now disintegrating nest of branches.

David, with great self-control, had not jumped straight in after his twin, because he knew he might help more from the bank. He saw his mother trying to pull Sally—who was on her back, holding the possum in the air—out of the pool at an angle that would hit the hidden bank just before the main stream of the river took them. He threw off his jacket and waded carefully down, then leant forward, ready to take hold of them.

He could see that his mother was making a super-human effort, and they were getting closer. He leant even further forward, one hand clutching a tussock under the bitter cold water, and the other stretched out towards them. He could almost touch them, and then the bank gave way and the river rushed down and took all three into its fierce and freezing grip.

David dropped deep down. Like a biting pain, the cold entered his ears and eyes and bound him round his forehead. He kicked wildly, propelling himself up-wards. With a gasp he reached the surface and gulped for air. His mother and Sally were still quite close, but downstream, and his mother was looking back towards him. He saw relief on her face as he surfaced. Sally still held the possum above her chest and was swimming on her back, the brown water around her frightened face.

David put his head into the water and swam furiously towards them. The cold was too intense to keep his face in long, but he managed to get himself closer to them. He realized the speed of the flood because they were being fairly hurtled past the banks.

Joanna was trying to kick herself and Sally towards

the bank, through the rushing brown water, and he set himself to do the same, knowing as he kept trying to swim that the cold was making him so numb that it was becoming hard to move his limbs and that he was really being taken by the current towards the opposite bank. Now, indeed, there was nothing but the sound of the roaring waters in his ears. Then he saw that there was a huge fallen tree ahead of them. He gasped with fear. Nothing could stop them being washed against it, perhaps sucked under it, perhaps caught in its branches and battered by the force of the flood.

Joanna had seen it too, and knew that all her tremendous efforts to get herself and Sally out of the main current and near the bank were unavailing. They would crash into the tree.

For a moment she stopped swimming, and tried to see what, if any, part of the tree she could catch hold of. Then it seemed to be racing towards her, she felt branches under the water bruising her legs. With one arm still around Sally, she gave one tremendous kick and clutched a branch. There she hung on while the water tore at her and at Sally, who was caught in the lower branches and almost submerged.

'Quick!' Joanna gasped, heaving her up. 'Hang on and I'll help David.'

David had at that moment seen his mother catch the branch and hold on, and with his last strength he reached up for another branch above the stream and held it while his legs were fiercely sucked below unseen branches underneath the muddy water.

A log hurtled by, bruising his leg, but he held on

till Joanna could get close enough to pull him along the tree beside Sally.

Sally had found some sort of foothold, had pushed the terrified and soaked possum into her shirt, and was trying to climb up out of the water. If they could get through the branches without being torn away by the flood, there was a thick trunk to use as a rather perilous and steep path above the raging water to a high bank where the tree-roots still partly held.

They all clambered desperately up out of the torrent, Joanna going last, steadying and pushing. Their hands were blue and shaking, in fact they shook all over with shock and intense cold, but slowly they scrambled through the branches. Once David slipped and went waist deep into the water as he hung from a bough. He felt a complete hopelessness come over him as the current dragged at his body, but Joanna caught hold of his belt and helped him back.

The climb along the trunk to the bank looked to be almost the worst part. There was nothing to hold on to, and the great rushing flood beneath, waiting to claim anyone who looked down, got giddy and fell.

David went first, astride the tree, pushing himself up on his hands. He had no breath left in his body: the bitter cold and the force of the water had squeezed it all out of him and bound his chest with iron. Also he was shivering uncontrollably. Up he went, inch by inch, up the smooth grey and white trunk, gasping with the immense effort to move and the strain of not looking at the swift, dark water which drew his eyes over and over again and made his head giddy as it constantly rushed away. Once he lurched horribly over one side, but recovered himself.

Sally was just behind, and Joanna behind her. He could hear their voices in a blur, but Joanna's words suddenly became clear when she said: 'Not long now,' and he was sure her teeth were chattering. Sometimes Sally spoke to the possum. At last David could touch the bank with his toes, and he wriggled himself safely through the roots. The others followed.

'Hurray! Dry land,' Joanna laughed. 'Or nearly dry. Let's hope the horses are still there.' She peered down the front of Sally's jacket at the curled-up possum. 'He's all right,' she said. 'You were wonderful to keep him out of the water.' She patted Sally's shoulder, then added: 'Come on, we must move and get warmer.'

As she talked, the shaking twins began to feel better. She took each one by the hand and started to jog along in her stockinged feet, through the wet grass and tussocks, the pools of water.

'Lucky that tree was there,' she said.

David managed to control the chatter of his teeth and his sobbing breath to say:

'It was very bad luck that my piece of bank gave way. Otherwise I might have caught you both.'

'That's true,' Joanna agreed.

Sally felt her knees knocking together. She did not know how she was going to get back to the horses, or how she would ever ride home. The river had drained all strength and will power out of her. She felt so exhausted that she dared not say so, in case she cried.

The horses were close to where they had left them,

still standing, prick-eared and anxious, staring at the river, their reins trailing in water. Buckwong neighed as he saw them coming.

'Golly, it's cold!' David gasped as he sat on the saddle in his wet clothes. Then his face lit up. 'Why, Mummy! Sally! We're through Black Mag's roaring waters of the flood!'

'So we are,' said Sally, cheering up. 'And I never even thought of it.' She slipped one hand in to stroke the possum's wet back.

'I didn't think of it either,' Joanna admitted, though, looking at the pinched and frozen children who were trying to blow their noses on wet handkerchiefs, she wondered how well they were going to come through it. They would be lucky if their colds did not get far worse. Anyway, hot drinks and hot baths, and the pride of having saved the possum, might save them too, she thought.

'I hope the kingfisher feathers will dry out,' said Sally.

20 : Kangaroo road

THAT NIGHT the flood still roared around the house. Rain was falling again, and a bitter south-west wind blew. Joanna knew it was snowing on the Alps as she walked into the twins' bedroom and felt the freezing cold. The flood would drop.

She closed the south window and listened to the breathing of both children. It sounded heavy and distressed.

Sally turned over.

'I'm awake,' she whispered. 'Is the possum all right?'

'Yes.' Joanna bent and kissed her and felt the heat of her forehead on her lips. Then she switched on the lamp, looking at the flushed face, but Sally gave a sudden exclamation.

'Look! Look!' and there, blown against the west window, fluttering on the wire, was a robin red-breast.

David stirred and opened his eyes, seeing only the robin, bright against the night.

'He's here to tell us,' he muttered, and drowsed off, his breathing grating horribly.

Sally watched the bird with its black and white wings outstretched against the wire, its red breast shining, and its small head on one side as it gazed beadily into the lighted room.

'I wonder if the birds know we like them, the way animals do?' she said.

Joanna smiled as she went out of the room to get a thermometer.

Sally moved restlessly. She was so hot. The little bird on the window fluttered its wings again. David stirred and muttered hoarsely:

'The flood's roaring and roaring.'

'So it is,' said Sally. She knew that the flood was racing round the hill, but the noise in her ears was as though she were still in the grip of the flood herself. She sat up to get a handkerchief, and all of a sudden the room lurched and rocked. She lay down again very quickly.

'I do feel queer,' she said to her mother, as Joanna walked in with the thermometer. Then David started to cough and it seemed to Sally as if many things happened very quickly, but in reality it was almost an hour before the doctor first came out. Also it was not until the next night, at two o'clock in that pitch-dark hour, that their temperatures soared highest, and neither she nor David knew that the doctor was there at all. With the very high temperatures the roaring in their ears became louder, and they were sinking under the flood, sinking deeply, fighting for breath.

Outside the roar was subsiding as almost all the melted snow water had come down, and now it was snowing again on the mountains.

Sally and David were both far off in a queer land made of dreams and memories and of things that had not yet happened, a land that moved uneasily just as the room had lurched when Sally tried to sit up. They were together in this land, and yet each one dreamed it separately; sometimes talking aloud to each other, there in their own bedroom, so that Joanna and Alex heard them, sometimes only dreaming.

David had the highest temperature, and in his ears the roar was most loud, thundering, beating—the sound of the flood. Then through it all he remembered the old man on the mountain saying: 'Listen to the roar of the flood,' so he listened to the thunder and beat in his own ears, thinking it was the roar of the evil brown waters. Then he wondered why he had not realized before that there was a voice in the sound of the water, a voice roaring: 'Kangaroos! Kangaroos!' He tossed and tossed in his fever, sometimes crying out: 'Kangaroos!'

After a long time the sound died down in his ears and, in quietness, he found himself in a strange part of

o

the bush, where the kangaroos were hopping by, making the same shadow frieze in the dawn that they had made at Back Creek. David dreamed that he followed them on a track that led up a narrow spur. When the spur turned downwards he saw that the track went through a thick, dark belt of black sallee. The kangaroos went through, parting the old man's beard that festooned the trees like a curtain, and vanished. He turned to Sally, in his dream, and said:

'The cave must be somewhere in there.'

'Yes, come on,' said Sally, and walked through the dark curtain fearlessly, a strange smile in her eyes, as though she knew untold secrets.

Sally in *her* dream followed a robin that was flying above the snow. A little wind blew over the snow, rustling the stems of dried grass that still stood up. Suddenly she knew that the wind and the snow were whispering their secrets and that in some way she understood them though there were no words. The wind, and the snow, and the robin, the mountains and all the great bush would take her into their secrets. Then when she, too, found herself at the black sallee wood, she was unafraid, because somehow she possessed the secrets.

★   ★   ★   ★   ★

'This is the whitest frost I have ever seen,' Sally said. 'Look at the spider webs on the fences, the webs and the wire are all frozen white.'

'They're like blazing wheels if you get them against

the sun,' David said, and as he spoke a scarlet robin came, down the fence-line on the hill, flying from one white wire panel to the next, and occasionally hopping on to a white thistle and swaying there in sunlight.

David suddenly stopped still and kicked at a frosted tussock with his rubber boot.

'I wonder how well we did come through the test of the flood?' he said. 'D'you think we'll ever see the Dragon-fly Cave?'

'Well, we didn't drown, and though we were pretty sick, we're still alive,' answered Sally. 'I think we may find it, but we'll have to search!' She was watching the robin as she spoke, and David with a sudden shock of surprise saw an expression on her face that he remembered seeing when he was dreaming his feverish dreams—the strange smile as though she knew untold secrets.

'We have the sketch map that Tony Bell drew for us,' Sally went on. 'We'll just have to persuade Mummy that we are well enough to go to the bush again.' She watched the robin flitting along the fence. 'I'm sure the robins will have something to do with that cave.'

When they got back to the house for school work Joanna had all the books set out on the dining-room table, and a big back log was burning in the open fire-place. She was stooped over the table as they came in, her fair hair falling forward over her face.

'Was it lovely out?' she asked, looking up.

'Beautiful,' they answered together. 'Mist frozen on to cobwebs, and wire and thistles,' said Sally.

'And a robin,' said David, 'like a phoenix on a thistle.'

'I have read you a poem that describes those webs and wires—more than describes them,' Joanna said.

'Yes.' David spoke slowly. 'I can't quite remember it.'

'See if you can find it while I just finish working this sum.' She bent her head again and Sally and David went to the shelf of poetry books. After a few moments there was a shout from David.

'I've found it!' he cried and read out aloud from one of Judith Wright's books:

> 'When I was a child I saw
> a burning bird in a tree.
> I *see* became I *am*,
> I *am* became I *see*.'

Then he skipped some verses and found the one he was looking for.

> 'The sudden sun lit up
> the webs from wire to wire;
> the white webs, the white dew,
> blazed with a holy fire.'

Joanna, watching the two eager faces, realized they were well again, and surprised them completely by saying:

'Twins! It's time we went searching for the Dragon-fly Cave!'

'Yes, oh yes,' said Sally, hopping on one foot.

'When?' cried David.

'Tomorrow, while the weather lasts.'

David's eyes sparkled.

'We shall have to leave very early, if we are to see where the kangaroos go.'

Sally was so excited that it was impossible for her to stay still.

'You're right,' she said. 'We must leave here hours before daylight, in the freezing cold.'

So it was arranged. Joanna and Alex were certain of the place at which Tony Bell had meant them to stop the car and take off into the bush. His little map showed them the way they had to take, and they had a rough idea of how far they would have to walk, but that was all. The exact whereabouts of the cave remained a mystery.

Sally was sure it was in a cliff, and she did not know why she was so sure, only that she had a picture in her mind of a rock cliff above a stream, and a robin red-breast perched on a rock. Alex felt that if a cliff existed there, Bell would have known of it. Both children were adamant that they would have to go through a sombre and weird black sallee wood.

'Dawn comes at a quarter to seven,' Alex said at lunch-time. 'We should leave here at four-thirty. There's about one hour's drive: it'll take us a few minutes to gather our gear together, and then we want to get into the bush towards the little plain where the 'roos graze before it gets light.'

'I hope there's not a mist,' said David, almost trembling with excitement.

There was a mist next morning. When they woke up, the twins immediately looked out of their window. They could see bright stars in the sky, and the Southern Cross hanging over the valley of the Indi; they could see the white wraith of their lovely snow mountains—but the valley below was an inland sea, filled with mist.

Sally felt her skin creeping with excitement as she made a place in the Land Rover for the possum's box. What was the mist going to hide? What would come out of the mist? What would happen today? It was weeks since they had heard anything of Black Mag and sometimes the whole thing seemed to be a dream of their high fever.

When they drove away from the dark house, with the cold eating into them, the mist was rising, enveloping car, road, fences, muffling the noise of the engine and the hollow sound of a bullock lowing. Up on the Gap they were above the mist and the stars were bright overhead. They dropped down into it again, and from then on, for many a mile, the mist lapped around them, mysterious and sinister.

Along a low-lying part of the road, a hollow in the hills, the fog was so dense that they could only creep. Then wet fog froze on the windscreen and Joanna stopped the car for David to get out and scrape it off. The silence was intense and David found himself continually looking over his shoulder as he scraped at the glass. He could see nothing, of course, nothing but the all-encompassing wall of darkness against which the headlights were simply reflected back, and the low foglights made very little impression. He, too, felt his skin creeping.

There was intense silence which was suddenly broken by a sound. Muffled by the mist, yet close at hand, came the unmistakable rattle of sulky wheels and the clop of a horse's hooves.

'Black Mag,' whispered David. Sally and Joanna both jumped out of the Rover, but before they could speak she was there, swathed in mist, almost invisible, as though the fog was thickest where she was. They could all feel her eyes on them, and then out of the mysterious fog came her voice:

'I am the last. I am the last. I have seen you in all my nights. I have seen you passing through many dangers, but still I have not seen you at the Dragon-fly Cave. Without the feather of the blue bird you would never reach it, but you have the feather. Now find the cave and you will be part of the spirit of the bush, brothers to the birds, brothers to the beasts, brothers to the willy-willy that blows wild across the land— even the snow mountains will be your brothers.'

Alex Dane was leaping out of the car too. He had seen her and heard her, and he could swear she was real, but the mist and the night flowed even thicker into the hollow. The wheels rattled and moved—and she was no longer there.

'Well!' said Alex.

'Well!' Joanna echoed. 'You saw her and you heard her. We all did.'

'Yes, we all did,' he said. 'But she's certainly not here any longer.'

'Come on,' said David. 'Let's try to find the cave.'

They drove on in silence, each one thinking deeply. Soon they rose out of the mist and climbed up and up in the range which divides the Murray and Mitta Mitta valleys. At last Joanna said:

'This must be where we stop.'

'Yes,' said Alex. 'This must be it.'

Cramped and cold, and still rather silent, they got out of the Rover, put on their light packs, and Alex led off, lighting the way with his torch. Sally carried the possum inside her jacket. No one spoke after they left the road.

David was rigid with excitement. Soon the kangaroos must go by, he knew it.

On and on they walked. Once they heard a faint thump, thump, thump of something hopping ahead. Once the torch beam picked up a kangaroo's still form quite close, and then the grey animal went hopping away into the dark, in the same direction in which they went. David felt disappointed. He had been so certain that his dream must come true.

They walked for an hour on what was undoubtedly a bush animal's track, or perhaps on a series of tracks, and then, whispering very softly, Alex told them that, as far as he knew, they were on the Kangaroo Plain and in the general area of the Dragon-fly Cave.

Just then David felt Sally clutch his arm. A faint light had filtered through the bush and they could see, hopping obliquely across the way they had been going, the shadow frieze of kangaroos.

The four Danes stood watching.

'Quick! We must follow,' whispered David. 'We'll never keep them in sight.'

The kangaroos were not going fast, and they were stopping to graze, or stopping, with forepaws uplifted, to smell the rich scent of the mountain peppermints in the dawn air. The Danes could not always see them, but then they would catch up to the herd when it stopped to eat, and see them go off again—leaping, lovely grey shadows.

The twins were beginning to get tired, though they hardly realized it, and Joanna, who had looked at her watch when the kangaroos first appeared, knew that they had followed them for almost half an hour, which meant about a mile and a half, and knew that they were right within the area marked by the young surveyor as the place where the cave must be.

The kangaroos started up a long narrow ridge, and David, following, slowly became aware that he knew this country already. The ridge turned down and Sally whispered in his ear:

'The black sallees must be down here. Hurry!'

Down below, in a hollow, there was indeed a black sallee wood, dark and eerie in the half-light. David saw it. Shivering slightly, he put his hand in his pocket to feel the case containing his kingfisher feather. He wished that both his mother and father had feathers too, for had it not been whispered, by the light of the Brolga Moon, that the kingfisher feather guards from evil? The black sallee wood looked evil, and even more so as they drew closer and could see the hanging curtains of grey-green fungus. Since Joanna had been included in Black Mag's sayings, David wished she was adequately protected.

Then the kangaroos went hopping through the swaying curtains of old man's beard and black sallee branches—and vanished from sight.

David shivered again and held his feather tight. It was then that Sally walked forward and went first after the kangaroos.

In the wood they were once more in the blackness of the night, and the dark air felt heavy and difficult to breathe. Cold, frosted fungus touched their hands, their faces. One thick curtain, icy cold, swung back and hit David's cheek. He almost screamed. His father switched on the torch again, but it could not penetrate far through the wood, and it only made the fungus look white and even more ghostly, as it swayed slightly on a breeze which they could not feel.

There were no kangaroos to be seen, but their tracks showed in the soft black earth. The four searchers followed the tracks across the hollow, stooping below the dark branches, shying away from the sinister touch of the old man's beard. Even Joanna jumped with fright when a cold tendril swung round her neck.

By the time they reached the other side of the dark wood they were all taut and nervous—except perhaps Sally. David hastened out of the wood with the ridiculous feeling that someone or something was just going to clutch him from behind.

Dawn had really come while they were in the dark wood, and now the sun rose swiftly to gild the world of frost—and the four Danes found themselves on the edge of a steep drop. They gazed out over a narrow cleft and a small, glittering ribbon of frozen waterfall that shone on a wall of rock. There, right below the head of the valley and the waterfall, the kangaroos were hopping, visible for a moment only, below the rocks, and then gone.

When they turned down to follow them, they were on a well-worn track.

'Kangaroo road, I think,' said Joanna, and Sally was watching a bright robin that flew ahead through the bush, perching first on a limb and then on a broken sapling.

'There's a string of rock pools in the valley,' Alex murmured. 'Queer that Tony didn't say anything about this place.'

When they got down into the valley the kangaroos had gone completely. There was no sign of even one footprint, and no further track.

'Must have gone up rocks somewhere,' Alex said, and led the way up past the rock pool at the foot of the ribbon of waterfall.

'Hullo!' said Joanna. 'The stream goes under the rocks from this pool.'

'I think it goes underground more than once in this little valley.' Alex's face was alert and eager.

Sally was studying the ground all around them.

'The kangaroos could have crossed on these rocks without really leaving a sign,' she said. 'The rocks do look rather worn.'

All the time they climbed up the other side of the valley she kept staring at the rock headwall, hoping she would recognize it, but nothing seemed to fit the half-remembered picture in her mind. When she looked down she realized how still and quiet the valley was. The robin and the kangaroos had gone. There was no stir of life.

For half an hour they searched back and forth on the valley sides, thinking they might find tracks on the earth, and then they searched on the cliff for any sign of the kangaroos, hoping they might just happen on the cave. Then Joanna suggested that they were all getting tired and hungry and that they should go down and boil the billy and have some food before starting to search again. Perhaps, she pointed out, the kangaroos had, after all, turned downwards, and they might find their tracks down below. So they went leaping down in the early sunshine, running down the blaze of morning light.

The twins stopped only for a moment at the first rock pool, then ran on down to the next. There they went much slower, bent over as though sniffing for tracks. At the third pool Joanna announced that here they must stop. There was wood for their fire, and the bright shaft of sunlight reaching into the valley in which they could sit to warm themselves.

Sally and David collected sticks and bark. Soon there was the lovely smell of burning eucalypt, and smoke rising in a slender pillar out of the valley.

'Enchanted water to drink,' said Alex, filling the billy at the pool. 'Water from the valley of the Dragon-fly Cave—or is it the valley of the cave?' he asked the twins, half laughing.

'I don't know,' said Sally, 'but I think it is.'

'*I* think it is,' David murmured.

'Do you mind if you don't find the cave?' their father asked.

'We'll keep on looking, if we don't,' David grinned. 'After all, we're pretty sure that such a cave exists. I feel as if I am sort of brother to the birds and the beasts already,' he admitted suddenly, 'but it would be exciting to find the aborigines' cave, and I'd like to feel I belonged more to the mountains and the snow.'

Joanna whispered something under her breath:

'Part of the spirit of the bush,' and the others half heard her but said nothing.

While the billy boiled the twins went wandering around the pool seeking tracks or anything of interest. It was Sally who suddenly pounced on something and held it in her hands, gazing at it.

'What've you got, Sal?' David sprang towards her.

'I think it's the same,' she said, pulling her kingfisher feather box out of her pocket.

'Another kingfisher feather!'

'I think so.'

They compared the feathers and were certain that this was the wing feather of an azure kingfisher, and they ran back with it towards the fire.

'This may or may not be magic water,' said Sally, 'but here, I am sure, is a magic feather.' Ceremoniously she handed it to Joanna. 'For you and Daddy—the feather of the blue bird, found by the third pool in the valley of the cave.'

Joanna lifted the feather out of Sally's cupped hands as though she were receiving a wonderful gift.

'I shall wear it in my hair, and you two must wear your feathers too.' She clipped it to her hair and fixed Sally's for her, and then threaded the quill of David's through his jersey. 'Now,' she said, smiling at their father, 'we will walk close together to be guarded by the same feather.'

They drank their tea and ate hot sausages and bread-and-butter while the sunlight was getting stronger and warmer, and Sally gave her possum a banana. Sudden hope rose within them when the wonderful song of a plump grey thrush filled the air, and a robin red-breast flitted around.

'The bush has come to life,' said Sally. 'It was so quiet before, even though the dawn had come. The thrush is lovely!'

'Listen!' said David. 'There goes a kookaburra.'

'And I can hear kurrawongs in the distance,' said Joanna.

Sally got up and rinsed the mugs at the pool.

'Back to the cliff now,' she said.

'Don't you think we should try down the valley before going back?' her father asked.

'No,' Sally answered. 'Let's try the cliff once more.'

David looked up at the headwall.

'Everything is going to look different now. We have the necessary feather: the bush has come to life: the way to the cave may be visible.'

The thrush went on singing as they walked up the

valley, and high overhead an eagle hung in the shining air. The eagle was still there, poised above them, as though watching, as they climbed up a place in the rocks that had that indefinable look of being a track even though the rock was too hard to wear.

Joanna, with the feather in her hair, was walking behind the twins.

'I'm sure wallabies must come this way,' she said, 'or even kangaroos.'

Both the children turned and smiled at her and the sunlight glinted on their feathers too. 'Kangaroo road! I'm sure it passes the cave,' said David.

As they went on, Sally, with the possum on her shoulder, suddenly shot ahead.

'Look! There's a robin.' Her whisper floated back, and there *was* a robin, flying from one rock to another, ahead of them.

Alex spoke from behind.

'This looks different, we didn't climb just here before.'

The robin perched on a flat cliff face for a full thirty seconds, and then flew away out over the valley. Sally and David climbed up to where he had last perched. They could see nothing that looked unusual, just flat rocks fitting closely against each other. Sally put her hand up to the top of the rock on which the robin had sat, and found her fingers going round a fine-cut edge. She drew in her breath sharply.

'What's up?' asked David.

'The robin rock seems as if it's only a shell.'

'Oh.' David sprang up beside her.

Then they were squeezing, one after another, behind the rock into a small, sandy corridor beyond.

'Can you get through?' Sally asked her mother anxiously, as Joanna's face peered round the crack.

'By going up and over we can, I think,' Joanna answered, and soon she and Alex were beside them.

The corridor inside the rock was lit by the early sun in one long shaft through a hole in the ceiling.

All four hastened along the narrow passage, silent-footed on the sand. Then Sally gave a shout! The corridor had opened out into a cave. Another shaft of sunlight fell straight on to a painting of a dragon-fly.

'We've found it!' cried Sally, and she and David ran forward. Joanna saw them both illumined by the shaft of sunlight, with their kingfisher feathers shining blue and the possum nestling against Sally's neck. Then there came a movement of the air in the ceiling of the cave, as though a breeze suddenly blew up above and came funnelling down through the hole in the roof.

'Listen!' whispered Sally, and they heard the voice of the old aborigine woman coming through the hole in the roof.

'The greatest prize . . . part of the spirit of the land, brothers to the birds, and the beasts, to the great trees and the small flowers, to the willy-willies that blow, to the snow that softly falls.'